A COWGIRL'S LOVE

BARRELS AND HEARTS SERIES BOOK 5

EDITH MACKENZIE

A Cowgirl's Love (Barrels & Hearts #5):

Images © DepositPhotos – Alan Poulson & Khunaspix

Cover Design © Designed with Grace

❀ Created with Vellum

For my Dad hopefully watching down on me and hopefully getting a kick that I actually did it. Thank you for being my Dad xx

Chloe stared at the picture of the bull staring back at her. Trust Travis to have that as his profile picture. She could imagine him sitting down at a battered old desk, scrolling through the pictures on his phone, trying to decide which bull picture he liked best. She giggled a little at the thought as she quickly typed in a message and attached the pictures of a growing Nova. Teeny was still too young to have her own account, so Chloe sent everything about the young horse via her father. Not that she had a problem with that at all. In fact, it gave her the perfect excuse to stay in contact with him—regular contact.

"You almost finished?" Deb asked, trying to look over the pretty young blonde's shoulder.

Chloe quickly hit send, realizing too late that she had made several errors. *He's going to think a fifth grader sent it.* Giving a little groan, she turned to face her friend. "You know, it's rude to read over someone's shoulder."

"Oh, was it personal?" Deb's eyes were wide in feigned innocence as she popped a piece of gum in her mouth.

"No, I was just sending some pics of Nova to Teeny." Chloe held her hand out for Deb to share.

Handing the packet over, Deb's eyes sparkled impishly. "Oh, so it was personal then. You were sending a message to Travis." She made a kissing face as she said his name.

Chloe could feel her face heat up as the blood rushed to the surface. She was about to deny it when Gabi, Frankie and Megan entered the bunkhouse. *Dang it, I forgot we had a meeting this morning.*

"Talking about Travis again?" Megan asked as she settled herself into her customary chair, her belly already starting to show.

"What makes you think we're talking about Travis?" Chloe asked, giving the chuckling Deb a dark look.

"Well, you only ever get that particular shade of red when you're either talking about or to Travis." Gabi winked at the others as she placed her laptop on the table.

"Aren't you going to help, Frankie?" Chloe pleaded, mortified at the conversation that swirled around her.

Frankie laid a sympathetic hand on her shoulder. Gratitude that someone was finally going to put a stop to this discussion flashed through Chloe and she sent a smug look to the others.

"Welcome to the club, kiddo. All I can say is, it'll be painful. They have a lot of experience and stamina as far as teasing about this particular subject. Stay strong and, eventually, you'll get used to it."

Chloe looked up, shocked at her idol's betrayal. "That's it?"

"That's it." Frankie calmly sat down. "Now, what's on the agenda for today's meeting?"

～

THE BATTERED pickup truck and horse trailer pulled up in front of the barn, loud music blaring only slightly louder than the raised girls' voices that emanated from the cab. Deb cast Frankie a doubtful look. "Not a great start."

"It'll be fine," Chloe said, looking anxiously at Frankie's unimpressed raised eyebrow.

The doors of the truck groaned open, the springs giving a squeak as the weight inside shifted, and the occupants stepped out. "That is not half," Ash said. Well, at least Chloe thought it was. It could be hard to tell Ash and Savannah apart just by looking at them. But Ash tended to be the fierier of the two.

"I don't even have to share it with you. I'm the one that spent my money buying this candy bar. I didn't see you offering to pay." Savannah slammed her door shut with great gusto and stormed to the front of the truck.

"We're sisters. We share everything." Ash, not to be outdone, slammed her door ferociously as well, charging to meet her sister.

"No, you borrow everything of mine and never return it." Savannah wrinkled her face up, clearly not agreeing with her sister's sentiment.

"That's not true, and we're not talking about that right now. We're talking about this tiny bit of candy you gave me. The rules are you break it and I get to choose."

Savannah gave her sister a hard look, her mind clearly working. A crafty smile suddenly appeared and, without warning, she licked the candy bar in her hand. "There, now you can't have it."

"Please, as if that's going to stop me."

"Are you running a babysitting club now?" Deb enquired, eyes tracking the performance before them.

"Hey, they're my age," protested Chloe, china blue eyes wide in offense on behalf of her friends and at the idea that

Deb thought she was a kid too. At twenty-three, she felt quite worldly and mature, thank you very much.

"I don't remember you turning into an old lady." Frankie raised her eyebrow in mocking challenge at the snide tone of her friend.

"Hey, you're my age," protested Deb, echoing Chloe's earlier words.

"But I look good for it." A teasing gleam shone from Frankie's eyes as she shot her friend a sideways glance before stepping forward with Chloe to welcome the newcomers. "If you're quite finished ladies."

Identical auburn-haired heads turned at their approach. For the time being, the angry words were silenced as if suddenly aware they weren't alone. "Ah, hi, Frankie," the girls said in perfect unison.

Ash waved, looking embarrassed. "Didn't see you there. Hi, Chloe." She peered past them. "Hey, Deb." Deb just shook her head in disbelief and headed back into the barn.

"Get your horses unloaded and meet me in the arena in fifteen minutes," instructed Frankie. "Do you think you can manage that without yelling at each other?" She looked sternly at the girls.

"Yes," the twins answered.

"It's just that she didn't share the—" Ash began.

Frankie held up her hand for silence. "No, I don't want to hear it. Leave all of that at the gate. You're here to learn, and if you can't hear my words over your chatter, then you can get back in your truck and head home."

Chloe's eyes went round in shock. She had never heard Frankie sound so tough before. The twins looked equally stunned, their faces shaded with remorse. "We're sorry, Frankie," Savannah said.

"We won't let it happen again," Ash added.

"Well…" Savannah looked guiltily at her sister. "I mean, we can try."

"We can definitely try." Ash nodded her head in agreeance.

Frankie, nostrils flared, looked like she was seriously starting to reconsider her decision to begin transitioning into coaching. Or maybe it was just having the twins as her first regular pupils. Chloe wasn't exactly sure which it was at the moment. All she knew was that she had never met such big personalities as the twins, and she had been living and working around Frankie, Deb, Megan and Gabi and their husbands for years now. Things certainly weren't going to be dull.

"I need more coffee." Shaking her head in defeat, Frankie stalked back to the bunkhouse.

"Is she always so…" Ash waved her hands about, searching for the right word as they started to unload their horses.

"Dramatic," Savannah finished.

Her twin pointed a finger at her. "That's the word."

Chloe pursed her mouth, unsure how best to answer this. Surely, they knew they were the cause of all the drama this morning. "Um, Frankie might have been a bit surprised by the entrance you made."

Identical green eyes stared at her in consternation. "What do you mean?"

Chloe began to realize that her version of events and how the twins interpreted it were miles apart. "I'll go see if Frankie needs a hand with that coffee."

CHLOE HAD THOUGHT that the twins would have similar riding

styles. But watching them train under Frankie's observant eyes with Deb and Gabi, she was surprised at how different they were. Ash was very reactive. Although quick to handle situations, she nonetheless never seemed to prepare her horse for the next thing to happen. Though, she was skillful in managing what came her way. Savannah, on the other hand, was the complete opposite, setting her horse up well before, but got rattled when things didn't turn out how she anticipated.

Chloe grimaced as Savannah knocked down the same drum her sister had just knocked over, but for very different reasons. "If you could roll them into one body, you would have the perfect barrel racer."

"I never fully appreciated it before, but I'm beginning to think that Frankie has the patience of a saint." Clearly, Deb had still not gotten over the earlier events.

"I wondered where everyone went," Megan said, approaching the fence. "You know, it's not nice to leave the pregnant lady to do all the work."

"I thought you'd be used to it by now." Deb nudged her friend. "I mean, you ran the stud single-handedly for a while."

"Yes, and watched you put your swollen pregnant feet up and get fed by Sra Ana."

"It doesn't look like you've missed too many meal deliveries from Mae," retorted Gabi. "For some reason, she keeps missing my house when she does them."

"Well, you'd better start thinking about who's going to be doing my work soon." Megan rubbed her belly for emphasis. "Based on previous experience, you need to start now if you're going to have someone by the time I have this baby."

Chloe smiled at her friends' banter. When she had been growing up, these girls had been her idols. It still blew her mind that she was treated as one of them. "So, you're definitely not coming back to work?"

Megan shook her head. "Not in the role I was in. I think I'll have my hands full with Cabrera Junior and my vet studies. Obviously, I'm such an asset you'll need to replace me with a few people."

"Two, at the very least," Gabi said, looking intently at the arena where Frankie now stood talking earnestly to the twins. "And I think I've found them."

"You've got to be bloody joking," exploded Deb. "What have I ever done to you for you to punish me like this?"

Chloe hid her smile behind her hand at Gabi's confused expression. "I do like you," she spluttered. "I literally have no idea what you're talking about." Gabi turned to the other girls. "Do any of you?"

Turning back to the arena, Chloe watched Frankie pat each of the horses, clearly wrapping up the lesson, identical smiles beaming down at her from flushed, tired faces. Well, it won't be boring around here.

CHAPTER 2

*G*abi's face was flushed, her movements more bustling than usual. Chloe narrowed her eyes as she looked at her, waiting for her to settle herself down and begin the meeting. Her eyes dropped down to her friend's belly. Her mouth pressed together as she considered if Gabi might be pregnant too. Shaking her head, she quickly dispelled the thought. Probably wasn't that. But there was definitely something that had her in a higher state of excitement than usual.

"Okay, everyone's here. I have a few things to get through first and then I have something that's, um, I guess the only word is amazing to share with you guys." Gabi quickly laid out her notes on the table, the chair creaking as she settled her weight, trying to get comfortable.

Frankie set a mug of coffee in front of Gabi. "I mean it's all right, you don't have to over sell it."

Deb turned betrayed eyes to Gabi. "What, Frankie already knows what it is?"

"Luc too," Frankie offered, sitting down smugly, looking

ever so slightly superior in her possession of the yet untold news.

"What!" spluttered Deb. "How's that bloody fair?"

"They've always been the favorites," Megan noted, clinking her spoon against her mug as she stirred it.

"You know, if you let Gabi start, we can get through all the usual boring stuff and then she can tell us what it is, too," Chloe slyly said, patiently waiting for the impact of her words.

"Thank you, Chloe." Gabi's eyes blinked. "My usual stuff isn't boring. It's important that I communicate what's happening in a clear and concise manner and that's what I do."

"And bore us to death," grumbled Megan.

"You know, if I'm so boring, we can cancel this meeting and then you'll have to wait another time for me to tell you the exciting stuff." Gabi began to gather up her papers, brows drawn together in a threatening manner.

"Fine." Deb threw her hands up in the air in defeat. "But it'd better be worth the snooze fest I have to go through to hear it." Chloe tried to smother her giggle, not entirely disagreeing with Deb's sentiments.

Gabi looked around the table, pausing at each face, except for the smug Frankie, to give them a darkly offended look before slowly putting her papers back on the table. "Fine. It's only because this news is pretty amazing that I'm willing to forgive your hurtful words." Graciously, she nodded at each of them, regal as a queen. "First, I've officially offered Megan's role or, I should say, a role that covers most of what Megan did, but under the supervision of Deb, to Savannah and Ash Decker."

Although she had been anticipating the offer to the twins, Chloe still felt excited to have some girls her age starting at the stud. Judging from Deb's groan, she was alone in that sentiment. "I swear I'm a good person," Deb grumbled. "Why do bad things keep happening to me?"

"It might be the negative energy you keep putting out into the universe," Megan innocently suggested, her eyes guileless as she peered at Deb over the rim of her coffee mug.

"I'll give you bloody negative energy." Deb glared back.

Choosing to not give the pair any more attention, Gabi decided to continue. "I've also begun to work with a property developer for plans for the new training center. As soon as we can get the plan finalized, we'll submit to council for approval."

Chloe clapped her hands together. "I can't wait to see what you've got planned. It's going to look amazing, I know it."

"If you think that's exciting, then you better hold on to your hat." Her eyes sparkling mischievously, she glanced at Frankie. "Do you think we should tell them now or make them wait for being naughty?"

Frankie smiled impishly. "Hmm, I think if they promise to be good from now on, we can probably tell them."

"Fine, we'll be bloody perfect little angels from now on." Deb looked at Megan and held out her little finger. "Do you want us to pinky swear on it?"

"A blood oath should be enough." Frankie's laughter tinkled out from her. "At least then I'll know you're serious."

"Are you going to tell us or what?" Megan, getting fed up with the delays, jutted her jaw out mutinously.

"Do you want to tell them or shall I?" asked Gabi, looking questioningly at Frankie.

"I think I might like to tell them." Frankie pursed her lips. "That's unless you prefer to?"

"I think it's really yours and Luc's news, so you should tell them."

"But you did create the opportunity, so it's your news too."

Deb's head lolled back against her chair. "If someone—and I bloody don't care who—doesn't start telling me what this bloody news is, I think I might scream."

Obviously deciding she had strung everyone along as long as she could, Frankie leaned forward in her chair, her hands clasped on the table in front of her. Chloe found herself unconsciously mirroring the position. A quick glance showed her the others had as well.

"Okay, so thanks to our tenacious friend over here"—she gestured to Gabi, a gesture her friend humbly accepted as her due—"she has negotiated the rights to a film being made about Luc's and my love story."

Stunned silence greeted her statement before pandemonium exploded. Deb leapt up to her feet, her chair flying backward as she waved her arms in the air. Megan clapped excitedly, finding it a little more cumbersome to rise to her feet so rapidly. Chloe, from her position at Frankie's side, was able to reach over and wrap her in a hug. "Oh my gosh, Frankie," she squealed. "That's so exciting. Who's going to play Luciano?" Eyes wide, Chloe looked at her friend. "Who's going to be playing you?"

Frankie laughed at everyone's exuberance. "We have no idea right now. It's only at the very early stages. But I'm as curious as you guys to find out."

"Maybe you could play you," suggested Chloe.

"Yeah, nah." Came her quick rebuttal.

"Can you imagine?" Deb laughed. "You'd have to bloody follow her around on set with a bucket."

Chloe joined in their laughter but couldn't help but notice the speculative look on Gabi's face as she stared intently at Frankie. Maybe she'd better start getting used to the idea of being a bucket holder...

~

THE DOOR WAS plain and solid, designed to do the job it had been allocated in life to the best of its abilities without the need for frills or decorations. Chloe thought it suited Travis perfectly as she stood, hand raised, about to knock on the door. Raised voices from inside gave her cause to pause.

"Is that Mom on the phone?" One twin—she couldn't be sure from the voice alone—asked.

Apparently ignoring her sister, the other twin continued her conversation. "Yeah, Mom. Anyway, we can't come home this weekend."

Chloe could almost imagine the angry red creeping up the unheeded sister's face. "Seriously, Ash, is that Mom on the phone?" Ahh, then that must be Savannah talking. "Give me the phone!"

The muffled sounds of wrestling interspersed with grunts and shrieks made Chloe lower her hand and seriously contemplate getting back in her car. Maybe she could just send them a text and ask how they were settling in.

"Hey, Chloe. What're you doing standing out here?" Travis's voice made her wish the ground would suddenly open and she could disappear into the earth's dark depths. How stupid must she look? Standing there like a dodo on his doorstep. Mortified, Chloe wondered how long he had seen her there.

"Oh, I was just about to knock and then…" She gestured to the door. Travis quirked his eyebrow at the noises still emanating from inside.

"You'd think they'd be sick of squabbling by now. It feels like I have three kids, honestly at seven, Teeny is the more mature of them all." She could smell his earthy aroma as he brushed past her to open the door and gestured for her to precede him. He hung his hat on the hook. "Do you think if I asked Gabi or Frankie really nicely, they could find room for them in the bunkhouse?"

She wasn't sure if he was joking or not. The interior of his home was warm and inviting, little touches showing that a woman had once graced the home with her presence. Chloe could almost imagine Travis's wife looking at the same table she was staring at, picking the framed pictures to place upon it. She felt a little prick of jealousy that she shooed away.

Having gained the upper hand in the scuffle, Savannah claimed possession of the phone and began talking to her mother. Ash, seeing Chloe standing there awkwardly, waved. "Hi, Chloe. When did you arrive?"

"Just a little while ago, but you guys seemed a bit busy. I thought I'd see if you two are ready for starting at the stud tomorrow?" Chloe decided it was best not to share the unflattering comments Deb had made about being turned into a glorified babysitter.

"Super excited." Ash retied her hair into a ponytail, attempting to restore order to her person after the scuffle with her sister. "Savannah, you've been talking to Mom for ages. Hang up so we can talk to Chloe." Her twin's face turned sour at the unfounded criticism and Chloe was shocked when she meekly bid farewell to her mother and complied. Ash patted the sofa for Chloe to join them. "So, what should we expect?"

As Chloe filled them in on life working at the stud, she found herself surprised at how much she was looking forward to hanging out with the twins. The other girls were nice and everything, but they were older and she sometimes felt like the kid sister. It was going to be fun to have girls her own age around. It didn't hurt that she had a crush on their uncle, either. She shot a guilty glance toward the kitchen where Travis was getting dinner ready. Perhaps sensing her look, he glanced up and smiled when their eyes met. For a moment, Chloe thought her heart was going to stop. Embarrassed the feeling might have showed in her expression, she looked to the ground. Yep. Travis being their uncle didn't hurt at all.

CHAPTER 3

Over the following weeks, the twins settled in. Chloe thought it added a new, fun dimension to the ranch, even if she was alone in her opinion.

"What?" one twin demanded of her sister, hands on her hips angrily.

"Nothing," the other responded, hands on hips as well, the perfect mirror image of her sister. Chloe wasn't sure who was who as this was the first time she'd seen them this morning. Usually, she could ask a few discreet questions to find out which twin was which and then make note of what each was wearing.

"I can feel you judging me," came the sharp retort.

"Savannah, leave Ash alone." Deb gave the second twin a warning look, clearly not in the mood for their bickering this morning.

"I'm Ash," came the indignant reply. If anything, her hands became ever more aggressive in their position.

Deb heaved the long-suffering sigh that Chloe half suspected was her new way of breathing since the twins had started at the stud. "I swear I can't tell the two of you apart."

Matching vexed green eyes flew to each other before snapping crossly back to Deb. "We look nothing alike," they said in unison.

Deb looked to be having some kind of internal struggle, verging on a fit, judging from the angst on her face. Her eye twitched slightly as she made a choking, strangled noise. Chloe wasn't sure if she should laugh or offer assistance. Regaining her composure, Deb turned to Chloe.

"One day, I'll get Gabi back for this. Till then, they're your problem." And she left her to deal with the two of them.

CHLOE FOCUSED ON THE RHYTHM, keeping the one-two steady, calming the horse beneath her as he attempted to speed it up in his eagerness to reach the drum. "Easy, Sam." With a flick of his head, he broke into a lope, pulling her forward. Sitting her weight down heavily in the saddle, she returned him to a jog again and turned him away from the barrel.

"Good," Frankie called from the side of the arena. "He needs to wait for you. He's so busy trying to rush in that he isn't letting you set him up correctly. He's young and thinks he knows everything, but what he needs to learn before we can train him on anything else is to listen." Chloe gave a nod, sweat dripping down into her eyes from the exertions of working the boisterous colt. "Okay, he seems steadier now. Try it again."

This time, she managed to keep him from breaking out of a jog and, although the pace was uneven, at least he tried. "Reward him," Frankie instructed. "Remember, we always reward effort. Even if it was 10%, we reward him, make a fuss. He needs to know that he did a good thing by trying."

Chloe gave Sam a hearty pat on the neck. "Chloe, you can start cooling him down. I think that's enough for him today." Frankie turned toward Ash, watching intently as the girl rode her horse in a large circle. "Okay, Ash, show me what you've got."

Chloe slowly walked her horse around, watching as first Ash and then Savannah put their horses through their paces. Frankie had started getting the twins to help Chloe with training the first crop of horses that had been bred at the stud. Although all had been sired by outside stallions, it was nonetheless exciting to have stud-bred horses coming through, ready to start their riding careers. Deciding Sam had cooled down enough, Chloe slid down from the saddle and headed for the gate where Gabi had been watching the training session.

"Sam made you work hard in there today," Gabi said by way of greeting.

"Yeah, he's all action and no brains right now. But once his brain matures a bit, he's going to be a really nice horse. Maybe not world champ nice, but he's going to make someone really happy doing local events, probably win an amateur quite a few jackpots." Chloe wiped at her face, looking forward to a nice cool shower soon.

"Cool those horses down and then you lot are done, too," Frankie called, making her way over to join Gabi and Chloe.

"How're they going?" asked Gabi.

"The girls or the horses?" Frankie rested an elbow on the top rail, squinting against the glare of the sun.

"Both."

Frankie cast an appraising glance over the twins and then Chloe before returning her gaze to Gabi. "Casper, Jay and Mickey, no chance they'll be ready for a while. It might actually be best to turn them out again for another few months and let them mature a bit." She looked at Sam grazing, the bit chomping as he tried to eat the grass around the metal in his mouth. "This one might actually benefit from some hauling, even if he spends it tied up to the side of the trailer. Jazz, Spritz, Monty, Rose and Shiraz should be ready to start hauling to some of the local events."

"What about the girls?" Chloe held her breath at Gabi's question. She'd been in the States for over a year now, and this was the closest she'd come to an opportunity to compete. She wasn't sure if the thought filled her with dread or excitement, and that surprised her.

"With a lot of work and some luck, each of those girls have the potential to replace me one day as a world champ. It'll just depend on how much they want it. We can supply them with world class horseflesh, and training"—Frankie jerked her head toward Gabi—"and you can help them get sponsorship, but it won't mean anything if they lack the fire in their bellies."

Chloe turned her attention inwards and tried to find the flame that Frankie obviously felt was so important. She wasn't sure if she possessed it or not. Concern filtered through her that maybe she would let them all down if she couldn't find it. Deciding that she would work hard and train the horses that were in her care well, surely she could just find it along the way.

ONCE THE GIRLS started hitting the road every weekend to haul to events, the weeks flew by. During the week, Chloe worked hard training the horses either self-directed or, when Frankie was in town, under her supervision. Usually, by Friday lunchtime, they were packing up the trailer and heading out to whichever event was on that weekend. For an only child like Chloe, it felt like she was now constantly in the company of the twins, which could be challenging for even the most stouthearted. Honestly, she wasn't even sure if Ash and Savannah knew they squabbled half the time, it was so ingrained. Finding herself craving peace and quiet, if only to hear her own thoughts, she made an excuse that she wasn't sure they'd even heard over their bickering and escaped to explore the rodeo grounds.

Aimlessly wondering around, she noted the condition of the surface in the arena—a little uneven—and how close the crowd would be sitting—fairly. A few of the young cowboys smiled when she wandered past as if hopeful to impress her later in the evening with their prowess. Her aimless drifting took her behind the chutes, her eyes searching until she saw what she had unknowingly been looking for the whole time.

Travis was standing watch over his bulls, his broad shoulders filling out his plaid shirt, his white straw hat gleaming in the early morning sun. He had the most unbelievable presence. Not flashy like Luciano, but solid and practical. Whenever Chloe was around him, she felt like, no matter what happened, he was immensely capable of handling it.

"I thought you might be hiding back here," she said as she made her way over.

He smiled as she approached. "I was waiting for a pretty girl to show up and now you're here, so it worked."

Chloe was taken aback. Was he flirting with her? His words sent a strange but not entirely unpleasant shiver down to her soul. "Um, speaking of pretty girls, where's Teeny?"

A faint smile still lined his lips as if he was amused by her attempt at redirecting the conversation. "She's off with some of the other kids running amuck. She'll be back when she gets hungry, I imagine."

"I didn't know you came to these little events now that you're doing the big-time rodeos."

"One of my younger bulls has just recovered from an injury. I want to see how he handles being on the truck again and how he's handling this event. That's why I'm out here now. Just giving him a final check to see if he's settled in all right." Travis gave a shrug, "Everyone knows that if a bull ain't ready now to perform, it's a little too late."

Chloe nodded as she listened. "I never realized, but it makes sense. Kinda like horses."

"Yeah, my top bull, Buttercup, wasn't too happy when he got left at home and Marshmallow got put on the truck." That sexy smile ghosted his lips again. "Old bulls always get jealous when the young ones get all the attention."

Chloe had a sneaking suspicion that he was talking about more than just cattle. "The old ones know they have nothing left to prove. Anyway, isn't Buttercup still in his prime? It's not like he's ready to be put out to pasture."

Travis's eyes searched her face intently. A flutter settled in her belly, and she wondered if maybe she was reading the signals all wrong. "I think some days he must feel older than others, especially when I put him in with a herd of young'uns."

"It's probably good for him. Reminds him that he's not as old as he thinks." It felt like he was trying to skirt around a question. There was something unspoken in the air. He took a step forward and Chloe's breath hitched in anticipation.

"Finally, we found you." Ash's voice shattered the moment. Chloe could quite happily have slapped her friend at that moment as Travis greeted his nieces. "Anyway, Chloe, some cute boys have asked if we want to sit with them to watch the rodeo."

"Well, the beginning, until we need to start getting ready to ride," Savannah amended.

Chloe looked regretfully at Travis. "I should get going. I hope Marshmallow goes good today."

"Me too. Chloe?"

She hesitated, hopeful. "Yeah?"

"I hope you go good today, too."

Smiling to herself, she followed her friends back to the grandstands, absurdly pleased at his well wishes.

CHAPTER 4

*S*he sunk gratefully into the welcoming embrace of her duvet, the bed soft beneath her. She drew in a deep breath, her chest lifting as her lungs filled to capacity, before slowly releasing it again. Chloe closed her eyes and drank in the wonderous sound of silence. No bickering, no loudspeakers, just the sound of birds and the gentle swoosh of her curtains in the breeze. For two months, she'd spent every weekend traveling and she was heartily over it. Ash and Savannah seemed to thrive on the constant hum of activity at the rodeos—it almost drove them to higher competitive heights. But Chloe had come to the recent realization that she was a homebody. Sure, she had enjoyed competing at the rodeos back home, but here in the States, it was next level. She felt like she could never relax.

Whenever she returned to the relative peace of the ranch —relative, because she still had to listen to the twins argue during the work day—she was reminded of how much she got a sense of completion from working with the horses, patiently waiting for the improvements to come. She had felt similar when she'd helped Frankie with the kids at the clinic.

Chloe snuggled into her pillow. All of that was tomorrow's problem. Tonight, she would luxuriate in the comfort of home.

~

"I think that's everything. So if no one else has anything they would like to add, I think we can finish up this meeting and get back to work." Gabi gathered up her things, already anticipating the answer.

"Um, I have something I want to talk about." Chloe half raised her hand hesitantly, feeling like a nervous schoolgirl about to ask a dumb question in front of the class as all eyes focused on her expectantly.

"Yes?" Gabi encouraged, her hands stilling.

"You know how grateful I am that you guys have given me the opportunities you have…" She picked at the cuticle of her nail, stalling.

"Are you going to tell us you want to leave?" Frankie guessed. She looked to her friends around the table for support. "I knew this day would come eventually, and I told myself I'd be brave and supportive of her decision. I am being brave, aren't I?"

Deb gave her hand a little squeeze. "Very brave."

Chloe had a feeling that if she didn't regain control of the conversation, it would spiral off in a direction that had absolutely nothing to do with what she wanted to discuss. "No, that's not it." She shook her head, blonde hair swaying with each empathetic shake. "That's not it at all. What I was trying to say is that I'm very grateful for the opportunity you guys have given me to compete here in the States. So many of my friends back home would give their eye teeth for the chance I have."

"I still feel like she's trying to break up with us," muttered Megan.

"I'm not trying to break up with you, I'm trying to say that I don't want to compete anymore. I'm not really enjoying it. What I really want to do is focus on training horses and people."

The impact of her words on the table was stunning in the polar opposite reactions it caused. The twins began to bicker almost immediately. Ash threw her hands up in the air. "She's breaking up with us."

Savannah gave her an accusing look. "What did you do to make her want to stop coming with us?"

Ash looked offended. "I didn't do anything. Maybe you did something."

Savannah sucked on her bottom lip, eyes worried. "Did I do something, Chloe? I wish you'd said something. I didn't know. I'm really sorry." The words skittered across the table to her.

Across the table, Chloe's bosses sat remarkably calm, quietly watching the twins twist themselves up into knots. "You guys didn't do anything," Chloe reassured the twins. "I thought I wanted to compete. In fact, I thought I wanted to be just like Frankie." She threw a rueful smile at her idol. "But it turns out that, once I started to go on the road, and I know we didn't even do it full time, but I realized it's just not what I want to do or where I want to be."

Frankie smiled, accepting the truth in Chloe's words. "Being on the road is a hard life, especially if you don't have your heart in it. There's nothing wrong with being able to admit it's not for you. In fact, I admire you for saying something now, before we committed more resources to you being out there. You're a talented horsewoman, and with more experience, I think you'll be quite successful as a trainer. Personally, you have my support and I'll help you anyway I can." She looked to Gabi, waiting to see what she would add.

"There's more than enough work training horses here, and we have more youngsters coming on all the time. In a few months, Nova and the rest of her foal band will be ready. And I'm sure, once Frankie's facility is completed and she's holding clinics regularly, she could do with your help over there as well."

"Definitely," Frankie agreed, sending Chloe an encouraging smile.

"Savannah, Ash, it's going to be just you guys hitting the roads on the weekends now," Gabi said, once again gathering up her things in preparation for leaving. "I expect you guys to be on your best behavior now that Chloe isn't there to separate any fights."

"Yes, Gabi," came the synchronized reply.

"Hey, Chloe?" Deb said as everyone stood.

"Yeah?"

"Looks like you might still end up being like Frankie after all."

"I can't believe you'd do that!" Ash exploded as soon as they were out of earshot of the others. "Why'd you throw away being on the road with us like that?"

"Yeah," agreed Savannah, her mouth downturned. "I thought we were friends."

"We are friends, guys," Chloe reassured them. It was true, they might drive her crazy with the constant drama, but they didn't mean anything by it. It was as natural to them as breathing. She briefly wondered if they had argued in the womb as well. "I just want to be home doing my own thing with the horses. I like knowing I'll be in my own bed each night."

"But what about all the hot cowboys? You'll be missing out on so many cuties." Ash's eyes opened wide as if horrified by the thought. "Quick, if you go back in and tell them you've changed your mind, I'm sure they'll let you keep coming with us."

Chloe wasn't going to be swayed. She didn't want a cute boy. What she wanted and had found was a serious, hard-working cowboy—a cowboy that came complete with a family. Now she just needed to get him to see her the same way. Thinking back to her last conversation with Travis, she amended that thought. Maybe he already did. And she was going to find out, one way or another.

CHAPTER 5

The gold foil balloon shaped like the number seven danced playfully on the end of its string. It had been quite the day at the ranch when the twins had hand-delivered all Teeny's birthday invitations. Looking around, it was clear that everyone who had been lucky enough to secure an invite had accepted. Grace was running around with Teeny playing tag with Senhor Eduardo as Sra Ana watched on, smiling at their exuberant display. Mitch and Deb were deep in conversation with Frankie and Luciano. Further along, Chloe could see Joao standing quietly with an animatedly gesturing Gabi, Carlos nodding at his sister's words as he stood attentively beside a seated Megan, her hands rested on her rounded belly. The twins had disappeared inside for the time being, and for now, Travis stood alone near the refreshment table. Deciding to seize her opportunity, Chloe tried not to look too hasty as she walked over.

"Teeny looks cute in her new dress." She smoothed away the hair the breeze had blown into her face.

Travis smiled proudly at his daughter. "It was a present

from the twins. I think it's the first dress she's owned for years. Usually, I can't get her out of her jeans."

"There's nothing wrong with jeans, but I like getting out of them as soon as I can." Embarrassment slammed hard into Chloe the second the words left her mouth. She could feel the heat creeping up her face and knew she was blushing. Travis's lips twitched, and he appeared to be exercising supreme self-control to contain his mirth. "I, um, that came out wrong. I meant that it's nice to wear something other than jeans once in a while." Chloe wondered that, if she prayed hard enough, the ground might open up and swallow her. Anything to get away from this blunder.

"I knew what you meant." She couldn't help but notice the admiring gleam to his eyes as his gaze swept over her. "I think you could wear a burlap sack and still look gorgeous." A wicked expression danced across his face as he leaned in a little closer. "I didn't mind the thought of getting you out of your jeans."

Chloe's mouth gaped open and she was amazed she didn't swallow any bugs. Her eyes flitted everywhere except directly at Travis's face as all thought fled her mind. She was warm all over, and an odd giddy rush went through her. Chloe tried to swallow her heart in her mouth.

"Everyone, gather around. It's time to cut the cake," Savannah directed as her and Ash carried out the birthday cake laden with candy bars of every description.

Chloe had never been so relieved and so disappointed to see chocolate before in her life. Teeny latched onto her father's hand as everyone gathered in close and began to sing happy birthday to her. Chloe thought she caught a look from Travis, but she was unable to decipher what his piercing gaze meant. She came back to reality while eating a slice of cake, which was quite delicious, and listening to the twins grill their cousin.

"Teeny, who's your favorite?" Ash asked.

"She doesn't even have to answer that. We already know it's me. Right?" Savannah wrapped her arm around the little girl.

Teeny looked between her cousins' expectant faces, regretfully shaking her head at them. "Neither."

The twins' eyebrows winged down as they turned to each other in confusion and then back to Teeny. "What do you mean neither?" they demanded in unison.

Teeny smiled up at Chloe. "Chloe's my favorite."

"But we got you that beautiful dress." Ash pointed at the article of clothing in question.

"And spent ages making that cake." Savannah gestured to where Chloe had a piece of the cake headed toward her mouth.

"Yeah, but Chloe's just cooler." Teeny smiled brightly up at her friend.

"Can't argue with that," Chloe said modestly. "When you're cool, you're cool."

"Chloe, can I show you something?" Teeny's small hand crept into hers.

"Sure thing, just let me put this cake down and I'm all yours.' Chloe was surprised when the little girl led her into the house and into her bedroom. An entire wall was covered in trophies and old pictures of a smiling young girl and then when the young girl looked to be a teenager dressed as a cheerleader.

"These are my mom's trophies. She was a cheerleader and really good. Her team was a national champion one year."

"Wow, she must've been amazing to win all these."

"Yeah, and I want to be like her. I want to be a cheerleader, too. It's not really Dad's type of thing, but." Teeny looked at Chloe, her eyes beseeching her.

"No, I don't imagine it is. Do you want me to talk to him and see what I can do?"

Teeny threw her arms around Chloe's neck. "Could you? Please get him to say yes."

~

"TEENY SHOWED me her mom's trophies."

Travis looked up at her words, his expression sad. "Yeah, she's convinced that she wants to be a cheerleader. I'm hoping it'll pass."

"I don't think it will. Why don't you want her to do it?"

"I don't have the time to run her into town for squad all the time. Once in a while, yeah, but I can't commit to two or three times a week. And"—he shoved his hands into his jean pockets—"I just feel funny sitting there with all the moms."

Chloe had a mental picture of Travis sitting in his plaid shirt between all the twittering women. She pressed her lips tightly together so as not to smile. "Well, I could take her, if you like?"

"I don't know. Wouldn't you prefer to spend your spare time doing other things, not chauffeuring to and from practice and sitting there?"

"I'm not really doing that much when I finish work, so I have a fair bit of free time. Especially now that I'm not traveling on the weekends anymore."

Travis wiggled his mouth as he pondered her words. "I'm tempted," he admitted. "I would like to see Teeny happy, and she's been at me about starting to cheer for a while now."

Chloe clapped her hands together happily. "It's settled then. As long as she knows that cheerleading isn't really a thing in Australia and I don't know a thing about it."

Travis looked at her gratefully. "You still know more than me. Except for the Dallas Cheerleaders—I know a bit about them. Teeny will be ecstatic when I tell her. She's going to think this is the best birthday present ever."

A warm feeling filtered through Chloe. There was something about the way he looked at her. The sense of being needed. If she wasn't careful, she could get addicted to it.

"JUST TO GET THIS RIGHT," Deb said, chuckling from the front seat as Mitch drove them home from the party. "You're now a cheer mom?"

"Maybe a cheer friend?" Chloe said from the back seat where she sat with Grace.

"Well, I'm going to expect you to start giving me more team spirit and pep at work from now on." Deb shook her head in amazement. "Of all the things I was expecting to hear come out of your mouth, that wasn't one of them. In a few weeks, you've gone from competing on the rodeo circuit, to quitting to stay at home, and now this. What next?"

"I don't know," Mitch commented as he drove. "Deb, I wouldn't mind seeing you in a cheerleader's uniform." He gave her a suggestive wink.

Deb looked back at Chloe in the rearview mirror. "Do you see what you've started now?" She looked back at her husband. "I think this is something we shouldn't discuss in front of the children."

"So, that's not a no?" Mitch ventured.

"No, that's not a no."

CHAPTER 6

The screen was full of fuzzy gray and black images. Chloe tilted her head to try and make out anything that she could recognize. Giving up, she turned to Carlos. Gabi, obviously having the same difficulties, rounded on her brother, hand on hip.

"Well?"

The vet continued to move the wand, ignoring the air of expectation that hung over the group. "I am pleased to announce that Affinity Stud can expect the arrival of another Delila and Sampson baby come the next foaling season."

"Well done, Delila." Frankie patted the buckskin mare's neck enthusiastically. "You're gonna have another little Sampson bub."

"I don't know, Nova gave her plenty of grief. Maybe it's best not to tell her till it's too late," Deb offered.

"I know I'm the one who wants to be the vet, but I thought you knew enough about biology to know it's already too late." Megan rubbed her back as she spoke, her belly now larger and obviously causing her some discomfort.

"Just like it's too bloody late for you," came Deb's tart

reply. "Hey, Carlos, how about we scan Megs next?" Megan simply smiled contently as Carlos began to rub her back for her.

Gabi clapped her hands together to get everyone's attention. "Okay, as exciting as this news is, we've all got things to do. Savannah and Ash should be finished packing the trailer now. Frankie, I'd check before you load up the horses and make sure they haven't forgotten anything.'

Chloe couldn't quite tell if Frankie smiled or grimaced at the thought of spending quality time alone with the twins while traveling to some of the bigger rodeos. "They probably got distracted by their arguing and haven't even finished packing yet."

There was almost a malicious enjoyment on Deb's face at the thought of Frankie getting stuck with Ash and Savannah. Or maybe it was just the idea of her getting a break from them. "You sure you're not regretting your decision? You know you and I are gonna be left to do all the bloody heavy lifting of running this ranch now," Deb asked Chloe.

"Not even a little bit." It was true—Chloe didn't feel the slightest pang at not going. Truth be told, she felt completely at ease with her choice. "Which reminds me, I need to go and get changed before I pick up Teeny for her first ever cheer squad." She waved at Frankie. "Good luck."

"For the drive, rodeos, or not hurting the twins?" Frankie raised her eyebrow in question.

"All of them."

CHLOE WAS surprised when Travis answered the door alone. "I'm real sorry, Chloe, but Teeny doesn't want to go anymore." He rubbed the back of his neck. "She's holed up in her room and doesn't want to speak to me."

She pursed her lips together, wondering what had happened to change Teeny's excitement from the previous night to sullenly hiding out in her room. "Do you want me to try and talk to her?"

Relief washed over his face. "Could you? I'm not sure what's happened."

"Sure thing. Maybe she just needs to have a girl to girl talk." Chloe headed up and knocked on the door. "Teeny, it's Chloe. Is everything all right?" Through the door, she could hear some muffled movement and then the click of the girl on the other side unlocking it.

The door opened a fraction. "You can come in now."

The last time Chloe had been in the room, she had been focused on the shrine of trophies. This time, she really looked around. The bed had a My Little Pony themed duvet on it. Well, at least what she could see of the linen had it. A mountain of clothes obscured most of it. The wallpaper had pink flowers that matched the pink curtains and the old rug on the floor. Posters of ponies and photographs of what Chloe assumed were some of Travis's bulls were stuck to the walls. Beside the bed was a framed photograph of a happily posing woman, smiling sunnily up at the photographer. Judging from the similarity with Teeny, it had to be her mother.

"I hear you don't want to go to cheer squad anymore."

Teeny stared down at her feet, scuffling them against the floorboards. "I can't tell Dad. He wouldn't understand."

Chloe sat down on the bed, uneasy that the conversation may end up in territory that she wasn't qualified to answer. "Wouldn't understand what?"

"All I have is stuff for the ranch and school. They're all going to make fun of me for not wearing the right things." A little sob escaped the distraught girl.

Chloe smiled, relieved that this was something she was

more than capable of handling. "Oh, honey, I know your pain. Every girl understands, trust me. One day, you should ask Frankie about never having anything to wear."

Teeny's eyes opened wide in disbelief that her idol could ever have such a problem. "Frankie's beautiful. Why would she ever worry about what to wear?"

"Every girl does at some stage. Now, let's see what we're working with here. I'm sure we can find something that'll get us through the first squad, and then we can sort it out from there.

THE FOYER WAS LINED with glass trophy cases, filled to overflowing with proof of the cheer gym's prowess. Girls ranging from five years of age through to teenagers scampered about in teal and white tops that stopped well short of their belly buttons and tiny lycra shorts. Atop their heads sat the biggest bows Chloe had ever seen outside of a horse show. She swallowed her nerves, determined to put on a confident front for Teeny, when she felt the girl's hand tighten on hers.

"Okay, we just need to find out where we need to go," she murmured, unsure if she spoke to herself or Teeny.

A preppy looking teenager stood behind the reception counter, talking animatedly on her phone. Chloe leaned against the counter and waited for her to notice her. When she did, she smiled.

"Hi, Catrina is starting new today in the mini squad. Is there anything you need us to do?"

The teenager tapped on the keyboard, waiting for the information to appear. "No, I have her paperwork already filled out and her fees paid." She smiled down at Teeny. "Are you excited to be joining cheer?"

"Yes, my mommy was a cheerleader, too." Teeny beamed up at the girl.

The girl flicked confused eyes to Chloe. "Oh, um, this must be your sister?"

Chloe smiled at the girl's bafflement. She hadn't actually thought how she would describe her relationship with Teeny to others. Luckily, Teeny answered for her. "This is my best friend, Chloe. She's gonna be here at all my squad training."

The teenager shrugged her shoulder, apparently accepting the relationship status from the little girl. "Well, that's nice. Now, Ms Ruby is going to be your coach, she's real nice. If you want to go in, she'll be starting the warmups soon."

Chloe smiled her thanks and, taking a deep breath and Teeny's hand safely in hers, she prepared for whatever was on the other side of the double doors.

A gaggle of young girls stretched and ran about, their steps giving dull thuds on the matts. A row of plastic seats had been set out and were filled with the other moms, their hair and makeup all uniformly perfect. Chloe knelt beside Teeny, a knot of apprehension in her stomach. "How're you feeling?"

"I can't believe I'm actually here." She squealed, bouncing on her feet excitedly.

A small platinum blonde who could have been twenty or forty—it was hard to tell beneath the layers of makeup— strutted into the room and clapped her hands sharply for attention. "Divas, lines ready for warmups."

Chloe gave Teeny one last reassuring smile and the young girl ran off to join the others. Casting her eyes about, she located a spare seat off to one side and made her way there. On her way over, she could feel the eyes of the other women drilling into her back. She tried to give a little smile, but none of them returned it. Self-consciously, she glanced down at her jeans and cowboy boots. Although clean, it looked out of place next to the dresses and jewelry the other moms wore. Noticing the long dramatic nails that adorned the women, she tucked her short, ragged nails under her legs and turned her attention to what was happening on the matt, knowing she was way out of her comfort zone.

Ms Ruby barked out orders as the girls jumped to her count, tucking their knees up to their chests before releasing them. Teeny was keeping up well. Chloe found it mesmerizing as they moved through the warmups and into practicing tumbling and then stunts. This world was so alien to anything she had ever experienced. The girls pulling their legs behind them in stunts, Ms Ruby calling out flyer and bases, arabesques, and basket tosses. Through it all, Teeny tried her heart out. Chloe was impressed with just how well the girl did for her first go. After the training had finished, she made her way over to where Ms Ruby was talking to Teeny.

"How did she do?"

"She did good, but I wouldn't expect anything less. I trained with her mother." Sharp eyes assessed Chloe as she spoke. Teeny beamed at the praise. "Now, she'll need to have the practice uniform before her next training. They are for sale at reception." And with that, she turned her attention to the crowd of waiting mothers. As Chloe shepherded Teeny out, she wondered what she'd gotten herself into.

"Daaaaadddddd!" shrieked Teeny, flying into the house and her father's arms. "Chloe bought me a training uniform and Ms Ruby thinks I'm good like Mom and I made so many friends and how to do handstands and some of the girls can do handsprings too."

Travis smiled at his daughter's enthusiasm. "So, you like it then?"

"I love it! It was amazing!"

"Well, dinner's almost ready. Go wash up." He stood from where he had knelt down to talk to his daughter. "You're more than welcome to stay for dinner. It's nothing fancy, but I made enough for you, too."

A jittery sensation shivered up Chloe's spine, chased by that familiar feeling of warmth he always seemed to cause when he was around. "Oh, if it's not too much of a bother."

The skin around his eyes crinkled as he smiled at her. "I think after how happy you've made Teeny, this is small thanks."

Long after Teeny had gone to bed, hugging her new outfit to herself as she fell asleep, Chloe lingered to help Travis with the dishes.

"I don't know what magic you did, but thank you for getting Teeny out of the house today. I didn't think she was ever going to leave her room again." Travis handed a plate to Chloe to dry.

"It was a girl problem. I don't think it'll happen again." She sucked on the inside of her cheek as she reconsidered her statement. "Actually, I can't guarantee it. In fact, you might end up having a lot more of those episodes. The good Lord knows I put my mom through lots of them." She laughed at the memories before sobering when she saw the look of sorrow on Travis's face. "I'm sorry. I didn't think."

A smile that didn't reach his eyes stretched his lips sadly. "It's okay. I feel guilty that Teeny is getting to an age that she needs a mom. She used to be my little ranch hand and always wanted to be around the bulls. She was always sitting on them, even the meanest ones, and it didn't matter what she wore as long as it was pink. Well, her mom used to buy her frilly little things before, well—" He cleared his throat. "It's been a while since she's had frilly things."

"It sounds like she loved Teeny very much."

"She sure did. Caroline and I were high school sweethearts. I never was the cool kid—the football player or anything like that. I had to work the ranch with my dad. And Caroline was the head cheerleader, but it never seemed to matter to her. When we found out we were pregnant with Teeny, well, I think it was one of the happiest days of our lives. I know it was of mine. The day I lost Caroline, well, I don't know if I'll ever feel that happiness she brought, the way she lit up a room, again."

It was as though the ghost of Travis's wife was in the room with them. Chloe felt intimidated by its presence. "I've never lost anyone. When I was younger, my horse died from a snakebite. I was devastated, and I know it doesn't compare to losing Caroline, but after a while, I could think about him and remember the good times and how I felt rather than the pain of him not being around anymore. I think Caroline would want you to be happy, not just for you, but for Teeny."

Travis's eyes were shadowed as he handed her another plate. Chloe wasn't sure if she'd made things better or worse. All she knew was that she had to try and ease his pain, an agony she felt as desperately as if it was her own.

CHAPTER 7

Chloe stirred her coffee dreamily, the spoon chinking on the side of her mug as the caramel tones swirled together. Last night, something had changed between her and Travis, she was certain of it. She just wasn't sure how much. Pondering how best to tackle the situation, she nearly jumped out of her skin when Deb closed a cupboard behind her.

"Bloody heck, Deb, you scared the living daylights out of me."

Deb chuckled at her reaction. "Considering I'd already said good morning to you, you must have really been out of it." She wiggled her eyebrows at Chloe. "Does it have anything to do with how late you got home last night?"

Chloe took a moment to comprehend what Deb was trying to imply, her mouth opening and closing like a fish suffocating on air when she did. "No," she denied hotly. "It was nothing like that. Teeny did really good at cheer after a bit of a rocky start and then, as thanks, Travis had made enough dinner for me as well. We just talked about how Teeny did and stuff." *And his dearly loved dead wife.*

"So how was it?"

"Dinner?"

"No. Cheer, you goose." Deb tapped her on the top of the head with the tea towel.

"The moms are next level. Like, not what I'm used to at all from back home. You should see them. Actually, scratch that idea, don't come. I don't think I can trust you not to say something. But Teeny loved it, and she was actually really good for her first go. What some of the more experienced girls can do is next level."

"Sounds full on." Deb splashed more milk into her coffee. "Are you regretting having made the offer to take her?"

"Nah, it's only twice a week. How bad could it be?"

Deb shrugged her shoulders as she took a bracing sip of her coffee. "I'm not sure, but I guess you're about to find out." A tiny worm of worry began to nibble at Chloe's confidence at her friend's words.

"AND THEN SHE asked if I wanted to be the flyer for an elevator. I was a bit scared, but then I did it, and I was so high I could see the top of everyone's heads." Teeny giggled at the memory.

Travis looked fondly as his daughter, perched comfortably on his rankest bull, Buttercup. The bull was mellowly chewing on some hay as she waved her arms excitedly with her tale. It made his heart sing to see her so happy, and it was all thanks to Chloe. His heart made a funny flutter at the thought of the beautiful young woman with her soulful eyes. Eyes that reflected her goodness. A young woman that a widower ten years older had no right to feel the way he did when he thought about her.

~

GABI'S MOUTH dropped open for the moment robbed of words as she read her email. Chloe's eyes narrowed curiously. It wasn't every day that her boss was lost for words. This should be interesting. Ahhh, there it was. The sudden, sharp intake of air as Gabi drew in air.

"No way!" she squealed. "I just, I can't deal. Wow, I can't believe they went with him. Luciano is going to be painful to deal with after this, but wow." Gabi's eyes were saucer wide, her color high with excitement.

"Do you know what she's talking about?" whispered Deb as she made lunch for Gracie. The little girl was practicing opening and eating her lunchbox in preparation for her starting elementary school soon.

"Literally not a clue." Chloe watched, amused as Gabi fanned herself with her hand, her giddiness infectious. "Okay, Gabi, we give. What's got you all hot under the collar?"

"Not what, who." She spun her laptop around. On the screen, a ruggedly handsome man peered out. He had the slightly weathered appearance of an outdoors man, crow's feet already appearing around his eyes as he squinted into the camera, a slight smirk hovering on his lips.

"No way!" exploded Chloe. "Kirk Cooper is playing Luciano?"

"Are you for real?" Deb practically drooled over the image. "I mean, I love Mitch and everything, but Kirk Cooper is like my all-time favorite actor and, dang it, he's one hot hunk of a man."

Chloe pulled her eyes reluctantly away from the screen. "So, who's playing Frankie?"

Gabi rolled her eyes heavenward. Clearly it was not going well. "That's the thing. They're having difficulties with casting her. I've been having talks with them, that if they can't fill the role, Frankie should play herself. They're actually quite interested in the idea. I just haven't gotten around to breaking the news to Frankie. If the producers decide they want to go with her, we would have to fly to LA for an audition, so it's best not to worry her until I know if they want to go down that avenue."

Deb looked steadily at her friend. "You know if they do decide they want her, Frankie is going to have a nervous breakdown."

Gabi quirked her mouth guiltily. "I'm sure if I give Frankie plenty of warning, she'll be okay with it." Chloe and Deb looked at each other and then exploded with laughter, pounding each other on the back. "Maybe she'll warm up to it in time," Gabi offered. Her friends simply laughed harder at her optimism.

CHAPTER 8

Chloe took a bracing breath, steeling herself for the walk past the other cheer moms. Teeny had already skipped off through the doors, eager to catch up with her new cheer friends. Deciding she couldn't linger at the doors any longer without looking like a creeper, she brushed down her shirt, pasted a smile on her face and determinedly walked in.

The same posse of women had claimed the prime seats, identically perfect in their appearances. Chloe kept her laser focus on the seat off to the side where she had previously sat. Her composure was temporarily rocked when she spotted a new lady in an oversized knit cardigan and faded jeans sitting slightly away from the group. Her face was gently lined and tired, but her eyes had a softness to them at odds with the rest of the moms. Chloe's spirits lifted at the notion that maybe she might be able to be friends with the newcomer. She sent her a smile and wave in greeting and the lady happily returned it, albeit hesitantly. Ms Ruby called the squad to attention and regret made Chloe's mouth downturned as she realized she had missed her opportunity to engage the newcomer in conversation.

"Excuse me, I don't think I introduced myself last time." Chloe looked up to find herself staring into the falsely smiling face of the woman she had dubbed head mom. She'd noticed last time that the others all deferred to her. "I'm Beth." The woman extended her hand. Polished red nails glinted like talons making Chloe feel like she was prey being stalked."

"Hi, I'm Chloe." Behind Beth's shoulder, she could see her potential friend keeping her eyes fixed on the girls training, her posture rigid.

"Oh, you're an Aussie, how cute." Beth settled herself on the spare seat between Chloe and the rest of the spectators. "I see your daughter is learning some of the tricks to be a flyer. That's quite advanced for someone only starting out. I hope Coach knows what she's doing, I wouldn't want to see her get hurt." Beth's eyes opened wide with insincere concern, her hand finding its way to her heart.

"I think Teeny will be fine. If she didn't think she could do it, Coach wouldn't ask it of her. Anyway, Teeny's mom was a champ." Chloe tried to focus her attention back on the floor where the girls were completing their warmups.

A sparkle of malicious interest gleamed in Chloe's unwanted companion's eyes. "Oh, so you're not her mom. We did wonder, since you seem so young."

"Yeah, I'm Teeny's friend."

Beth played with the large beaded necklace at her throat. "I see. You're the girlfriend." She nodded as if it now made sense to her.

Chloe began to feel like she was being interrogated but was too uncomfortable to decide how best to handle Beth's questions. "No, we're just friends."

"Well, isn't that a little scandalous. Some of the other

women will be mighty worried about letting you anywhere near their husbands. A young girl like you makes them nervous. A man can't be trusted to fight his baser urges."

Chloe's head whipped around at the carefully worded insult, denial hot on her lips. "No, I'm not like that. I mean, if I saw them at a football match or something when the girls were cheering, I would say hi, but nothing more than that."

Beth gave a slow laugh, the sound condescending as it tinkled out of her. "Oh, bless. I'm sorry, I thought you were being funny, but I see you're serious." She shifted her chair closer. "Our girls don't cheer for footballers or at games. Our girls are the athletes. They're the stars. What we do here is competitive cheer. I would have thought they'd explained that to you before you signed up. Maybe if you go to the front desk, you can tell them you made a mistake. It might not even be too late to ask for a refund."

Chloe felt foolish under the other woman's mocking. "I think we'll stay. After all, the coach seems to think she has potential. Is your daughter a flyer, too?"

Beth's features turned arctic. "Yes, she's the top flyer." Chloe looked out and saw Ms Ruby giving Teeny some pointers and a younger version of Beth, her face sour, looking on. "Oh, and the lady you seem to be trying to be friends with? She's only here because the coach feels sorry for her. I mean, look at her. Dirt poor and no husband in sight." Beth's face brightened as if she had a sudden thought. "Actually, maybe you guys have a bit in common." She rose to her feet. "Honestly, it still isn't too late to ask for a refund. I'd hate for you to lose money over a silly little mistake." As Beth walked by the newcomer, she deliberately kicked her handbag, spilling the contents everywhere. "That wouldn't have happened if you hadn't left your trash around."

Chloe, appalled at Beth's behavior, rushed to help the other lady gather up her possessions which, admittedly, were not that many. The woman smiled at her gratefully. "Are you sure you want to be seen helping me in public?"

"Completely sure. I'm Chloe, by the way." She extended her hand.

The woman hesitated, uncertainty written across her tired face. She tentatively reached out her hand. Chloe was absurdly pleased to see that her nails were short and raggedy just like her own. "I'm Sara."

"Well, pleased to meet you, Sara. So tell me all about this cheerleading gig."

ONCE AGAIN, Travis had dinner waiting when Chloe brought Teeny home. A pleasant homeliness filled her as she sat at the table, a simple, wholesome meal before her and glass of wine warming her belly as Teeny laughed and bubbled with her tales of squad. From time to time, she would meet eyes with Travis, both of their faces flushed with laughter from the little girl's stories. After Teeny kissed them both goodnight, Travis topped up her glass before repeating the gesture for his own. Once he returned the bottle to the table, he rested his hands comfortably behind his head, contentment plain in every ounce of his body.

"I can't remember the last time I've seen Teeny this happy. I mean, she's usually happy, but now, it's"—he held his hands apart, fingers splayed wide—"it's next level. She almost glows with it. I know I've said it before, but I have you to thank for that."

Chloe sipped her wine slowly, savoring the delicious way it slid down into her belly and left a trail of warmth behind. "She's a pretty cool kid. It's not that hard to want to do things with her." She gave a little groan. "You need to stop inviting me to dinner. I think I ate too much."

"For a little thing, you sure can eat. Actually, it's nice to have someone appreciate the dinners I make. Teeny doesn't complain, but she eats it cause she's hungry, not because she's a fan of my cooking."

Chloe patted her engorged belly, laughing. "No complaints here, except maybe that my jeans are too tight." She blushed as she recalled the last time they talked about her jeans. Travis obviously remembered too, his eyes darkening. Feeling flustered under the intensity of his gaze, she stood up. "I think it's time I head home and let you get some sleep."

Chloe could feel the warmth radiating from his body as he walked her to her car. When they reached it, he stopped intimately close to her. "Goodnight, Chloe. Sweet dreams." As he leaned down, Chloe's heart pounded in her chest, the anticipation building as his lips brushed her forehead, and then stopped as he straightened again. Quickly, she opened her door and started the engine, tears of disappointment and confusion blurring her vision as she drove away, uncertain if she was ever going to get the signals Travis sent right. Feeling like a foolish schoolgirl, she drove on into the night.

ra Ana placed the tray of food in front of Megan, steam spiraling delicately as it danced upwards. Chloe's mouth watered as her belly rumbled and reminded her that she hadn't eaten since breakfast. Gracie walked carefully in, her entire five-year-old being focused on the plate of cookies she carried to the table. Sra Ana placed her arm proudly around the youngster's shoulders.

"Gracie made these from scratch all by herself."

Grace puffed up her chest with importance. "I even cracked the eggs myself and didn't get any shell in the bowl."

"Well the proof's in the eating," Chloe reached a hand eagerly toward the chocolatey deliciousness that waited on the plate. They were gooey and rich, three different types of chocolate chips floating amongst it all. "My gosh, Gracie, these are amazing."

Megan quickly set her spoon aside and grabbed a treat, obviously scared if she didn't act fast, she would miss out. "Chloe's right. These are almost as good as Frankie's."

Gracie's eyes lit up. "You really think so?"

"Girl, I know so." Chloe paused as she reached for

another one. "Do we need to save some for when your mom gets back?"

"No, I promised I would make a fresh batch for Poppy Eduardo and Mom can have some from there." She looked up at Sra Ana. "Nanny Ana, do you think we should start on that next batch now?"

The older woman smiled fondly down at the girl. "Knowing your Poppy Eduardo, he will already be waiting in the kitchen for his cookies."

Carefully, Chloe swept the cookie crumbs into her hand as the two bakers left to whisk up more wonderous treats.

Megan sighed lustily, slurping on another spoonful of soup. "Seriously, this soup alone is worth getting pregnant for, let alone all the other bloody marvelous things Sra Ana keeps bringing me."

"Is Carlos a great cook as well?"

Megan smiled like the cat that had gotten the cream. "Almost as good as his mother." Guiltily, she looked around as if afraid the older woman had heard her. "Maybe don't tell her that though."

"What's my silence worth?"

"Chloe! I'm absolutely shocked that you would treat a poor pregnant lady like this." Megan feigned a strident expression, her spoon rattling into her bowl.

Chloe laughed. "It never hurts to ask." She looked down at the crumbs still in her hand. "Can I ask you something, Megan?"

Her friend's expression turned sly. "Sure, listening is free. But my advice is very expensive."

"Poor pregnant lady my foot," scoffed Chloe at the rapid reversal in roles. "Um, well, how do you know if a guy likes you? You know, like likes. Not just friends." She looked down again at her hand in embarrassment. She couldn't imagine the twins not being able to tell if a guy liked them or not.

Megan, for her part, didn't ridicule her inexperience. "I'm probably the last person qualified to give relationship advice. I need more information if I'm going to have any chance at giving you something helpful."

Chloe quickly filled her in on the previous evening and Travis kissing her on the forehead and all the little conversations that had left her confused but, at the same time, encouraged that he liked her. She felt relieved to finally bring her dilemma out into the light of day and tell someone.

Megan laughed, shaking her head in amazement. "Oh girl, have you got it bloody bad for Travis. I mean, I can see why that strong, older widower type is definitely attractive."

Chloe could feel her face burning at her friend's teasing, even if it was gentle. She raised her chin defiantly. "So, I like him, he's a great guy."

"Okay, so you bloody like him. Maybe instead of tying yourself up in knots about if he likes you or not, just ask him out," Megan suggested, polishing off the last of her meal.

Chloe, aghast at her friend's suggestion, felt sick at even the thought of laying it all out there so blatantly. "I don't know if I can do that. What happens if I twisted things around and he has zero interest in me?" She slid lower in her chair, horrified at the imaginary rejection.

"At least you'd know." Megan shrugged. "Honestly, that's all I've got. I'm not really good at these sorts of things." She reached for the last cookie. "Just remember, if you take too bloody long, you might miss out completely." And with that, she enthusiastically shoved the whole thing in her mouth.

IN THE TWIN beams of her car's headlights, shadowy bugs were highlighted before being extinguished. The plastic of the old steering wheel creaked beneath Chloe's hands, her grip tight as she grappled with her feelings. Cheer squad had been so much better. Now she'd found an ally in Sara, she hadn't felt the sick feeling of dread that she'd previously had on entering the lion's den. The other woman warned her that she was not making a friend of Beth and her group by continuing to sit with her. True to Sara's word, Beth and her cronies had spent the entire session giving them side eyes and laughing. Chloe wasn't entirely sure what they giggled and pointed out behind their cruel hands, but it somehow felt like she was dealing with the mean girls back at school.

The highlight of her day whenever there was squad was the now customary dinners with Travis and Teeny. Chloe loved the intimacy of the setting. Sometimes when she locked eyes with Travis, Teeny laughing and telling stories, she would pretend that they were a little family. Tonight, she had not been able to indulge in her fantasy. The twins had returned from their trip with Frankie and the calm, peaceful setting had been shattered by their bickering and constant attention seeking. It had been hard to be friendly to them while she battled her disappointment at not having the after-dinner one-on-one time she was craving.

Chloe shifted her grip on the wheel, her hands beginning to cramp from her white-knuckled grip. Thinking about Travis messed with her head so much. She alternated between excitement at the prospect of spending time with him, the mere idea thrilling to confusion and uncertainty when she did. She felt like a confused, awkward schoolgirl around her worldly teacher crush. Maybe Megan was right. Maybe she should just ask him out. If he rejected her, at least the pain would be swift and then over like ripping a Band-Aid off. Anything was beginning to seem better than this constant state of purgatory.

CHAPTER 10

The water droplets caught the light as they sprayed through the air, creating a rainbow. The mist was cool against Chloe's skin as she hosed down Sam, a moment of perfect solitude that ended all too quickly with the arrival of the twins, for once, in perfect harmony.

"Hey, Chloe. Savannah and I were saying that since we've been home for a while, we haven't had a chance to catch up with any cute boys."

"And it's ages till we go back out to any rodeos," Savannah added, tying Monty to the rail beside Sam.

"Isn't it like, two weeks till you're on the road again?" Chloe handed the hose over to Savannah and began to scrape the excess water off her horse.

"That's what she said. It's ages away." Ash dramatically rolled her eyes heavenward, as if questioning Chloe's hearing. "Anyway, we've decided what we really need is…"

"Girls' Night!" The twins shrieked in unison, causing the horses to stir uneasily at the commotion in their midst.

"Yeah, I'm not sure," Chloe hedged, hanging the scraper on the rail.

"Don't be an old lady. How long has it been since you've done anything but work, run Teeny around, and have dinner with Travis?" Ash looked at Savannah for her agreement, an affirmation her sister was quick to give. "You're the most old married lady I've ever met, considering you're young and single."

Chloe's spine stiffened at the comment. There was nothing wrong with not wanting to chase every hot guy that crossed her path. She wondered what the sisters would say if she said that the only hot guy she wanted to party with was their widower uncle?

~

CHLOE FELT like she was caught in a glitch in the matrix, the two images so identical it made her brain hurt. Black skin-tight sequin skirt, red lace off-the-shoulder top pulled daringly low, the tan fringed leather boots, even the exact same shade of lipstick. Chloe could feel her eye beginning to twitch as she took in the sight of the matching twins before her as she sat on Ash's bed.

"Ah?"

"Darn it, Savannah. I picked this out days ago. You need to change." Annoyance snapped from fiery green eyes as they both took in the other's outfit with hands on hips.

"I don't know who made you boss, but I'm not changing."

"Fine then, we can go matching," Ash suggested, suddenly all easy acceptance.

Chloe watched, fascinated as Savannah's mouth began to twitch, her jaw working. "Argh! I'm changing."

As she huffed off back to her room, Ash flopped down on her bed. "She's so dramatic."

Chloe wasn't quite sure how to respond to her friend's statement. "Well," she hedged. "I mean you both look great in that outfit, so I guess I can see why she would be annoyed to be the one to have to pick something else."

Ash smiled smugly. "It's okay. We have a killer snake print dress we both look hot in. Speaking of hot, dang girl, you look smoking. The guys are going to be falling over themselves to get your number."

Self-consciously, Chloe looked up at the mirror on the wall. She'd spent days agonizing over her outfit selection. Not for the potential hot guys at the club, but for the hope that Travis would be appreciative of her appearance. The black leather pants fit her like a second glove and the cut of her turquoise halter neck top was sufficiently daring to tease at what it covered without the fear of spilling out more than she bargained for while she danced. Finished off with strappy heels and her golden hair shining in loose waves, she knew she was guaranteed to attract attention.

The problem was, when she arrived earlier, Travis was nowhere to be seen. When asked, Savannah had informed her blithely that Travis and Teeny were out on a father-daughter date. Which was sweet, but didn't stop the surge of disappointment that he wasn't there to appreciate her effort.

Savannah strutted back into the room and executed a twirl in the exact outfit Ash had predicted. "What do you think?"

"I think you took ages and we could be there already dancing." Ash grabbed her things and looked down at Chloe. "Ready?"

"Ready." Seeing Savannah looking crushed at her sister's brushoff, Chloe smiled encouragingly at her. "I think you look amazing." She sent Ash a sly look. "Much better than the last one."

~

"You know you've just done the exact same dance moves for the last three songs?" Savannah yelled over the loud music to Ash.

"She's right." A random guy bravely entered the conversation, maybe hoping to earn brownie points with Savannah.

Eyes furious, Savannah rounded on the hapless suitor. "It's none of your business how she dances."

Ash, now entering the fray, was more brutal in her assessment of the situation. "If I wanted an opinion on dancing, I wouldn't ask it from someone whose dance floor highlight peaks at hopping about side to side like some sort of demented pogo stick."

"She's totally awesome at that move." Savannah continued her diatribe. In the face of identical wrath, the would-be boogie critic slunk away, his tail well and truly between his legs.

Chloe laughingly shook her head at the display. Ash and Savannah might fight like cats and dogs between themselves, but heaven help anyone who dared to say anything negative to one in front of the other. Then it was on like Donkey Kong. Waving to get the girls' attention, she gave a drinking gesture asking if they were ready for her to buy the next round. Enthusiastic nods set auburn curls bouncing.

Weaving her way through the packed dance floor, she eventually made her way to the bar after fending off several overly friendly pats on her backside and even more requests for her number. Taking up a position on the edge of the bar, she was able to see across the full length of the horseshoe-shaped counter. In the opposite corner, a couple were making out, lost to anything but each other. Chloe wasn't sure where to look as everyone beside them began to stare. Finally, they stopped their passionate display. More from lack of breath, she suspected, than any awareness of the attention they had been receiving.

The guy was obviously no stranger to the gym and was attractive in that buff, bicep-bulging kind of way. He had a baby face that seemed at odds with the rest of his heavily tattooed body. Chloe was shocked to discover the woman he had been making out with was much older. She would almost put money on the guy not being the woman's husband. There was something vaguely familiar about her. Chloe leaned harder on her elbows on the bar as she tried to get a closer look at her. The blonde's hair was disheveled, her lipstick smudged, and eyes blurry. Chloe's mouth dropped open in shock as her brain finally registered where she knew her from. Far from her usual immaculate self, Beth stared, her eyes threatening as she looked across the bar at her.

TRAVIS WASHED his hands in the kitchen sink, admiring the bright sun of the early afternoon that beamed in through the window. He topped up the coffee in the percolator and switched it on.

"Seriously, do you need to be so loud?" groaned the lump on the sofa that he now identified as Ash.

"I think I'm dying," agreed Savannah from the floor beside her.

"Sounds like you guys had a big night. What time did you end up getting in?" Travis asked, pouring himself a cup. He reached for two more mugs. Judging from the groans still coming from the living room, they were going to need it.

"Um, we stayed till they closed." Savannah answered, sitting up as he handed her the coffee. "It was epic. You should've seen all the hot guys asking for Chloe's number. She was on fire."

Travis felt a twinge of unexpected jealousy at the thought of guys hitting on Chloe. He tried to tell himself that he was being stupid, that he had no right to feel that way. She was far too young for an old guy like him.

"It's no wonder. She looked smoking hot last night. She totally wasted it but, not giving her number to anyone and then leaving just after midnight. When I asked her why, all she did was smile and say none of them were her type," Ash complained. "It was like she thought she was Cinderella. I mean, what does she mean, *not her type*? A hot guy's a hot guy."

"Right now, I don't care, Ash. My head's killing me." Savannah pulled a cushion over her head in despair.

Travis smiled into his mug, absurdly pleased that she hadn't been interested in any of the young bucks, and hummed happily to himself as he left his nieces to their misery.

CHAPTER 11

"I don't know what you did to Beth, but whatever it is must be huge." Sara leaned in, her eyes enormous at the possible causes Chloe could have given the catty woman to have created the current reaction from her.

"Trust me, Sara. You don't want to know." Chloe sighed miserably and slunk lower in her chair, trying to focus on Teeny trying to perfect an elevator with the help of her bases rather than the beastly woman sitting with her cronies and giving her filthy looks. She could feel from the loathsome gazes piercing into her and from their pointed laughter whenever she so much as glanced in their direction it was clear she was once again the subject of their conversation.

Chloe looked at the clock on the wall again. Thankfully, there were only a few minutes till the session was over. After what felt like the world's longest five minutes, she began to say her goodbyes to Sara. An excited Teeny ran over, thankfully coming to a stop before she ran Chloe over. "Chloe, Ms Ruby wants to talk to you. She thinks I can be a flyer full time."

Chloe waved a goodbye as Teeny dragged her out onto

the matt and to the waiting coach. "Teeny said you wanted to talk to me?" She always felt like a school kid when Ms Ruby looked at her. It was unnerving.

"Yes. Teeny has the build and, I think, the potential to be a flyer, but she's raw. She needs to practice if she wants to really reach that potential, and to do that, she needs someone that will help her. If I start training her with more skills to be a flyer, I need to know that she's working on them at home." Ms Ruby skewered Chloe with an intense look. "Can you commit to that?"

Chloe swallowed, awkward under that gaze. "Um, yeah. I mean, I don't know how much help I'll be, you know, since cheerleading isn't really my thing. Teeny knows more than I do."

"From now on, I want you to come fifteen minutes early and I will get one of our senior girls to run through the tricks with you and what you should be looking for." Ms Ruby's tone brooked no argument.

"Yes, Ms Ruby."

Teeny laid the last fork on the table as Chloe added the glasses and Travis set the plates heaped with steaming stew down. "Anyway, so then Ms Ruby said to Sue Ellen—she's the girl who's the head flyer now—that sometimes I'll be practicing her tricks." Chloe groaned inwardly, knowing that Beth would not take lightly to anyone learning her daughter's tricks, let alone Teeny. Next squad was sure to be fun. "Ms Ruby says it's a big responsibility and I need to practice. She made Chloe promise she would help me train more at home."

Travis's forehead crinkled, his eyes uncertain. "Honey, Chloe is busy too, she might not have time."

Chloe waved his concerns aside. Now that the twins were back on the road and it wasn't foaling season yet, once her workday was finished, she had spare time and nothing to fill it. It didn't hurt that it meant she would be spending her free time over at Travis's ranch. "I wouldn't have agreed, Travis, if I hadn't meant it."

"Well, as long as you're sure." He poured wine into her glass before doing the same to his own and settling down at the table.

Before long, Teeny's excited chatter slowed down and, except for the contented chews around the table, silence prevailed. It was a change from when the twins had been there. The youngster yawned, trying to stifle it behind her hand as she scraped up the last of her meal. "Okay, missy. Shower, brush teeth and bed for you," Travis said.

"But Dad," protested Teeny. "I'm not even tired." Another yawn escaping her lips proved her statement to be a lie and set her off giggling. "Okay, maybe I am." She took her plate to the sink. "I'll be back down in a bit to say goodnight." She scampered off.

Travis began to clear the table and Chloe rose to help him, carrying her dishes over. He reached out for them and their fingers touched. A jolt of electricity ran up her nerve endings, and her gaze flew to his face, eager to see if he had felt it to. Travis cleared his throat and looked away as he placed her plate into the sink.

"It's a lot quieter with the twins gone," Chloe said, trying to break the silence.

Travis smiled, relief breaking across his face, apparently just as eager. "You should've heard them moaning the day after y'all went out."

Chloe laughed. "I can imagine. Those girls party hard."

He turned on the tap and waited for the sink to fill. "They said you didn't stay the whole night."

"It's not really my scene. Lots of sweating, and throw in the drunk people. I mean dancing is fun, but as the night gets on and people drink more, they can get a little too friendly."

Before Travis could reply, Teeny returned, smelling of soap and toothpaste. Travis caught her up in a hug, giving her a kiss goodnight. "Night, Dad."

"Night night. Don't let the bed bugs bite."

Teeny gave Chloe a quick hug. By now, she was included in the night-time ritual whenever she was there. "Night, Teeny. You did awesome at practice today."

"Thanks. Night, Chloe." With one final wave, she headed off to bed.

Travis returned his attention to the dishes. The pot he was scrubbing was apparently extremely dirty, given his efforts. After a long while, he rinsed it and placed it in the drainer. "The twins mentioned something about a lot of guys hitting on you and wanting your number."

Chloe was taken aback, not sure how best to answer. "Yeah. I mean, they ask, but I'm not really interested."

"Why?"

There was something in his voice, some tone that made Chloe realize her answer was very important to him. She chewed her lip, afraid that if she was reading the situation wrong, she was about to make a fool of herself. Megan's words floated around in her mind. Deciding it was now or never, she took a step, closing the distance between them. "Because I don't want any of them."

Travis stood, rooted to the floor. "Who do you want?"

She wet her lips with the tip of her tongue, his gaze rivetted to her mouth. "I want you."

Before she could lose her nerve, she closed the final inches between them and kissed him. Chloe might have known that she wanted Travis, but she was far from experienced. She had certainly never made a move on a man before. She could feel the slight roughness of his lips as she tentatively kissed him, uncertain if she should end it. And then his strong arms were around her, pulling her in closer, not just returning her kiss, but taking control.

When he finally released her, she was breathless, a warmth having claimed her body. Shell-shocked from the emotions rocking her, she looked up at Travis, unsure what she would see in his gaze. The look he returned was smugly male, his eyes gleaming with hot possessiveness. Chloe's mouth went dry. Apparently she had her answer.

CHAPTER 12

Chloe backed out of the doorway to allow Megan to pass. "I'm not that big," Megan muttered as she waddled by.

"I might be young, but I'm not stupid enough to reply to that," Chloe sassed, dancing out of reach as Megan went to swat her.

"Come back here so I can get you," called Megan as Chloe ran out of reach into the barn, laughing.

Chloe felt almost giddy, happiness bubbling over from deep within. The ring of her phone drew her attention back to the present. Digging in her pocket, she extracted it to see her mother's name flashing on the screen. She looked at the time. She loved her mom, but once she answered that call, she knew she would be stuck talking to her for ages and she didn't want to be late for the first at-home practice she'd promised she'd do with Teeny. Nibbling her lip indecisively, she finally gave into guilt. "Hey, Mom."

"Hi, Chloey Bear. How are things?"

What followed after was a rundown of everything from Mack taking her mom to her first prize winner's check, to cousin Mary's ex-boyfriend's sister's stepson's father's nephew winning the woodchop at the local show, to if she needed new undies and socks sent over. Chloe had long given up contributing to the conversation other than the appropriate 'yep', 'really?' and 'no, I didn't'. But then her mother changed tack.

"Chloe, I love you regardless of what you do, but what are your plans?"

Chloe blinked at the unexpected question from her mother. "What do you mean?"

"Chloe, you've been over there for a couple of years now and I know horses are your passion, but now that you've decided you don't want to compete, maybe it's time to come home."

"I can't." The words were torn from her lips before she could think of a legitimate reason why she couldn't. A reason that didn't involve her telling her mom about the handsome widower she had kissed the other night. "I mean, I'm still chasing my dreams, but I've found out that it involves training more than competing."

"What about your degree that you spent four years getting?"

"Well, I'll still use that—at least parts of it. I really like working with kids and teaching them about training and how to be good horse people." It was true. She couldn't imagine being in a classroom and teaching, but there was so much that she could apply from her degree, and there were life skills that she knew she could tie in when she taught— things that could make a real difference. "Mom, I hate to love you and leave you, but I promised a friend I would help with something."

"Okay, I love you and miss you."

"Love you, too." Chloe hung up the phone, knowing

before she glanced at the time that she was going to be late. "Thanks, Mom," she muttered as she bolted for her car.

PRACTICE WITH TEENY had been fun with lots of laughing as they tried to figure out moves together. Chloe had never been so grateful for Google in her life as she watched videos when she wasn't sure what to do. She'd felt a cold sting of disappointment when Travis hadn't been around, but she quickly brushed that aside to focus on the job at hand. At dinner, he had been polite, if not more friendly than usual, leaving Chloe feeling off kilter. Sure, she hadn't expected him to sweep her into an amorous embrace as soon as he set eyes on her, but she had anticipated some sort of look, a hint that something had changed between them.

As she sat through a politely awkward dinner, Teeny obliviously carrying the conversation, Chloe began to feel the burn of shame. Maybe he thought she was the type of girl that threw herself at men. Head down, she peered at him through lowered eyelashes. No, he knew that she hadn't encouraged a single guy when she went out with the twins, so that couldn't be it. The shame dissipated with the awareness that he didn't think she ran about town. By the time Teeny said her goodnights, the confusion had left her feeling queasy.

Stressed, Chloe rounded on Travis as soon as they were alone with her, only feeling more upset as he averted his eyes and concentrated on doing the dishes. "I don't know what's wrong, and don't try to say there isn't anything because something clearly is."

Travis sighed and dried his hands before facing her. "You're right. You deserve better from me than to pretend like nothing happened. It's me. I shouldn't have kissed you the other night."

Indignantly, she glared at him, hands on hips. "Excuse me? Firstly, I kissed you. And secondly, didn't you like kissing me?"

His eyes burned bright with his denial as they locked on hers. "I liked it more than I had a right to," he growled, his low voice sending shivery goose bumps up Chloe's arms.

"Then what is it?"

"Darn it, Chloe. I'm too old for you. You should be with some young guy without a care in the world, having fun. Not some old guy like me who comes with baggage." Frustrated, he glared at her, almost daring her to deny the truth of his words.

Not to be intimidated, she matched his glare. "I don't see any baggage."

"No? What about Teeny?"

"I don't see her as baggage. I see her as a bonus."

"You're too young for this. You should be out partying with the twins, collecting phone numbers, being young and carefree. Not what I have to offer—school runs and lunches. That's what it'd be like with me. I can't give you exciting."

He was being so frustrating! Chloe didn't know if she wanted to hug him or throttle him. "Maybe you should ask me what I want instead of telling me. I'm a big enough girl to know my own mind." She stepped closer, daring him to look away. "I know what I'm getting myself into, and I still want to be with you."

A look of such heart-wrenching vulnerability and pain met hers that she almost dropped her gaze. The naked sorrow was too excruciating to bare. "I'm scared." His words were so soft that Chloe almost thought she had imagined them, if not for the naked agony that seemed to come from his very soul. "Losing Caroline nearly broke me. If I hadn't had Teeny, I don't know if I'd have made it out the other side alive. If I allow myself to fall in love with you and, in a few years, you decide you don't want us, that you're too young for this … it would kill me, and it'd devastate Teeny. I need to think about her, too." His eyes pleaded with her to understand, but at the same time to say he was wrong, that she wanted this too.

Chloe took his hands in hers, gripping them tightly, as if the strength of her hold could prove her commitment and feelings. "I care about her, too. And if I say I'm in this, well, I'm not going anywhere. Not now, not ever."

Travis squeezed her hands back, the connection bonding them together in that moment. "I believe you. Lord help me, I believe you. I don't know what you see in me, but I'm too selfish to refuse this chance to be with you, to be happy with you. But we need to take things slowly and discreetly. I don't want to tell Teeny till we're certain this is forever."

Chloe smiled, relief that she had been able to make him see that they were worth a chance washing over her. "I agree. I don't want to do anything that would hurt Teeny."

He pulled her closer, his hands warm where they rested on her lower back. "Thank you." He lowered his head and kissed her and, at last, the final pieces of confusion fled into the night.

CHAPTER 13

"Are you sure you'll be all right while I'm gone?" Carlos fluffed a pillow and put it behind Megan's back, her belly now seemingly at the limits of its elasticity.

Chloe had to smother a grin at the patiently exasperated look Megan sent her husband. "I'll be bloody fine. Chloe will be staying right here with me if you're that bloody worried." Chloe quickly nodded her expected agreement and Megan raised her brows for any further argument from Carlos. When his face screwed up ready to disagree, she simply ploughed on, not giving him the chance. "Anyway, your mae will be over soon for her soup delivery and you're only ducking into bloody town. Now come and give me a kiss and get going."

Carlos smiled ruefully as he obediently leaned down to give the requested kiss. "I'll keep my phone with me at all times. If anything happens or you need me to get anything, you call."

Megan patted her belly. "We're not going anywhere. Now scram." Laughing, she shook her head at Chloe when her husband finally left. Chloe was so happy that her friend had finally been able to let herself feel the security and joy she deserved.

"You guys are so cute. He's like a big teddy bear now," Chloe said.

"Cute and annoying. He still tries to tell me how sexy and beautiful I am." Megan rubbed her belly. "Can you imagine? He gets a twinkle in his eye and I tell him that him sweet talking me is what got me into this trouble in the first place."

Chloe was tickled pink at the image of an amorous Carlos trying to chase the heavily pregnant, completely over it Megan around the kitchen, all Latin charm and smoldering looks. Quickly on the heels of that mental image came another thought. "Imagine if you have a girl. He'd never let any guy near her."

"Oh, I can imagine. She would be his little princess. I'll deny it if you ever say anything, but it's kinda nice to be fussed over. If you think he's bad, you should see the Cabrera's. They're just about bursting out of their skin with excitement to meet this little one." Megan looked more closely at Chloe, her face wrinkled as if she was trying to figure something out. "Okay, spill."

"I don't know what you mean?"

"Don't give me the raw prawn. Something's going on. You're almost glowing. So, spill."

Chloe resisted the urge to give a girlish giggle. "Um, well, you need to promise not to tell anyone. At least not for now."

Megan held up her little finger. "Pinky swear."

"I guess that's good enough." Chloe took a deep breath, knowing that once she let these words free, there was no taking them back. It was official. "Travis and I are, well, we kissed and now, you know, we're just quietly hanging out."

"Chloe!" Megan squealed. "If I was able to, I would jump up out of this chair and hug you."

Chloe could feel her own face splitting in two, the happiness contagious. "I know, it's great." Her face sobered. "But we're being very discreet and just getting to know each other. It's early days."

"I bet Teeny is over the moon."

Chloe looked down at her hands. "We haven't exactly told her yet. We just want to make sure of how we feel about each other before we tell her."

"Chloe," Megan sounded disappointed. "Secrets, even if you have them with the best intentions, never end well. I know you guys are trying to protect her, but if she finds out before you tell her, it could blow up in both of your faces."

The happy brightness that had filled the room only moments earlier dimmed at her friend's words and Chloe had to resist the urge to shiver. Determinedly, she smiled. "We know what we're doing."

"I hope so."

The door swung open, relief breaking out over Gabi's face when she saw Megan and Chloe in the bunkhouse. "Hi, guys, are you going to be here much longer?"

Megan looked suspiciously at Gabi. "For a little bit, why?"

Gabi set her things down on the table, fussing with the edge of her phone. "No real reason. Just thought it would be nice to catch up." She headed to the kitchen to make a coffee. "So how's my niece or nephew treating you?"

Megan raised her eyebrow as she shared a glance with Chloe. "Good."

"Okay, Gabi. What was the hurry to see you?" Frankie bustled in the door. Megan's expression turned smug, obviously satisfied that she'd been right. Something was up. Chloe settled back in her chair, eagerly curious about what was going to happen.

Gabi held out the coffee pot. "Coffee anyone?"

"Of course I'll have a coffee. Now, are you going to tell me what's going on or do I have to get Megan to sit on you?"

"No fair, picking on the pregnant lady!" Megan objected.

"Let me just finish getting this coffee for you. How about you sit down?" Gabi stalled. Chloe was fascinated, the room had the tense feeling of being at a tennis match. Beside her, Megan obviously felt the same, her eyes glued to the unfolding drama.

"Do I need to sit down for this?" Frankie asked, looking alarmed.

"It might be best." Gabi set the coffee on the table and took a chair across from her. Frankie remained standing. Seeing that she didn't appear to be getting ready to sit down anytime soon, Gabi seemed to come to a decision. "The producers would like to see you."

"Okay, sure. But I thought I'd finished all my interviews with them when they visited for script research." Frankie's shoulders began to relax, and she sunk slowly into the chair.

"It's not for that. They were really happy with the information and insights you were able to provide. They want to do a screen test with you."

"A what?" Frankie began to look alarmed again.

"I think it's where they find out if the camera loves you or not," Chloe helpfully supplied from the sidelines. She was beginning to wish she had some popcorn.

"Yes, thank you, Chloe," Gabi said before returning her focus to Frankie. "It's basically what our helpful little friend over there said. Just a little test to see how the cameras respond to you."

"Why do they need to find that out?" Frankie said slowly.

"They want you to audition for the role of, well, you." Gabi leaned back, fearful of the explosion. Frankie appeared to be dumbstruck, her eyes wide, her mouth open. Gabi leaned forward, her face concerned. "Are you okay, Frankie?"

Slowly, Frankie began to blink, a pink creeping up her

neck and spreading, inch by inch, across her face. "No way. Not a chance." She suddenly exploded to life.

"I think you're being a bit hasty," Gabi soothed, hand held up as if calming a spooked horse. "I mean, who better to play you than you?"

"I think I'm the one that suggested that," Chloe murmured to Megan.

"I wouldn't say that too loud. Frankie might hold you responsible for this," Megan replied.

Back at the table, the action continued. "You can't make me do this," Frankie cried.

"You're right. But as your manager and friend, I think you should at least audition."

"But what if I get it? I'll vomit every day on set, you know I will." Frankie sucked in great gulping breaths. Chloe wasn't sure if she was going to sick or pass out.

Gabi stood to pat her friend reassuringly on the back. "Then we'll just write it into the contract that Chloe has to be on set with you." She smiled, her eyes sparkling slyly over Frankie's head to Chloe.

"Looks like you're up kid," Megan said.

"Looks like it."

THE DUST KICKED up in the air, flung by the bull's hooves as it bucked and spun. What the bovine lacked in experience, it more than made up for with its enthusiasm and brute strength as it strove to free itself of the cowboy upon his back. Joao whooped beside Travis as they watched Luciano ride.

"I think you have a good one there."

Pride filled Travis at the other man's word. If anyone should know quality bucking stock it was these two bull riders. "I've been trying to breed one like this for years. I think he will end up better than his sire, Buttercup, and he's out of a heifer that's by Humpty Dumpty. The bloodlines say he should only get better with age."

"Does Teeny still name them?" Joao asked as both men herded the bull out of the arena, Luciano rising to his feet and dusting himself off.

"Yeah, but the names are changing. This one's Elevator."

"That is a good name. It felt like he tried to take me up several stories," Luciano said as he caught the end of the conversation.

"I thought that's what she meant, too, but turns out it's some sort of cheerleading move." Travis raised his hat to wipe the sweat from his brow.

"That is why Chloe spends so much time at your ranch, is it not? The cheerleading?" Joao asked as they walked out of the pen and headed to the cool shade of the porch.

Travis looked away guiltily, busying himself with getting beers from the cooler. "Yeah, she's been great with Teeny and helping with all of that stuff." He didn't miss the suggestive look that passed between the two Brazilians.

"She is very pretty." Luciano raised his brows suggestively. Travis had to fight back the urge to snap at the Brazilian man. Of course he could see she was pretty. He wasn't blind. Anyway, Luciano was a married man and had no right to notice how pretty Chloe was. His flash of jealousy surprised him, and he calmed his irate, unwarranted thoughts.

"And he makes her dinner," added Joao, a small one-sided smile ghosting his lips as he returned his friend's look.

Travis felt himself grow hot under their speculative gazes. "It's the least I can do with everything she's doing for my daughter."

Luciano turned to Joao. "Notice he did not deny that she is pretty."

"I'm not blind. Of course I can see she's pretty. But there's more to her than that." Travis wanted to bite his tongue off as soon as the words left his mouth, embarrassed that he had let himself be goaded into a response by their teasing.

"You like her, then." It was more of a statement than a question from Joao.

"More than I have a right to."

"And she feels the same way?" Luciano asked as he sipped on a cold beer.

"Yes. We have been getting to know each other," Travis admitted.

"Congratulations," Luciano said, beaming at him. "She is a nice girl, but you understand that Frankie would be very upset if she got hurt. And I would not be happy if my Querida was to be unhappy."

Travis sipped his beer. "I understand. We're taking it slow. Teeny still doesn't know, and I'd appreciate it if you didn't say anything."

Joao looked baffled. "Why would you keep this a secret? You are single, she is single, you make each other happy."

"I just need to make sure. I can't risk Teeny getting hurt."

"Will she not be hurt if she finds out before you can tell her?" Joao pressed.

"But she won't, will she?"

CHAPTER 14

Chloe watched as Carlos's truck drove madly away from the vet barn. Moments later, Senhor Eduardo's truck followed. Her confusion lifted as enlightenment settled over her and she urged her horse out of the arena and galloped toward the barn.

"Deb! Deb!"

Deb's excited grinning face appeared out of the bunkhouse door, Gracie bouncing up and down behind her. "Have you heard?"

Chloe slid down from Jazz. "No, I haven't heard anything, but I just saw the younger and older Cabrera's trucks drive off like they had the devil on their tail. Does this mean...?" she left the question hanging.

If possible, Deb's smile got broader. "Yep. Looks like we're going to be meeting the littlest Cabrera soon."

A wonderous excitement filled her. "I can't wait."

THE PING of her phone drew Chloe's attention away from the

conversation at the dinner table. An awestruck gasp of happiness was elicited as she read the message. "It's a boy. Megan had a boy!" She read the rest of the message. "Mom and bub are doing well, and they've called the baby Edward."

"Senhor Eduardo will be chuffed that they have called it after him," Travis said, smiling at the good news.

"He'll be puffing on a cigar by now, no doubt," Chloe agreed. "Sra Ana will be beside herself with another baby in the family. I'd better buy a present and take it to them when I visit tomorrow."

"Dad, can we buy a present for the baby too?" Teeny asked.

Travis smiled indulgently at his daughter. "I think that's a great idea. Do you have any ideas what we should get?"

Chloe hesitated, fearing that she might overstep. "If you like, we could get a present together?"

She couldn't read his expression as he looked at her and she was just about to take her suggestion back when Teeny bounced happily in her chair. "That way we can get a really big present!" Teeny raised her arms high above her head. "Like, this big."

"Well, if we're going to buy a present that big, I guess you'll need me to take ya'll shopping." Travis looked at Chloe. "If you like, I can come and pick you up after Teeny gets home from school and we can head into town and pick something out."

There was something in his gaze, a familiarity that tied Chloe's insides up in knots. "I'd like that." She dropped her eyes so he couldn't see how flustered she felt when he looked at her like that. "I'd like that a lot."

EXPECTANT PARENTS AMBLED about as an orchestrated *Twinkle*

Twinkle Little Star played over the store's loudspeakers. There were sections for strollers and prams, furniture, clothing, toys, swings, and everything in between. Chloe, having never set foot in a baby store before, was completely and utterly at a loss at where to even begin looking for a present. Sighing in defeat, she turned to Travis who was standing beside Teeny who was busily trying out all of the rocking chairs.

"I have no idea what to get her."

Travis tilted his head as he pondered her statement before sending her a smile that caused her heart to flutter about in her chest. The smile that said he had utter faith in her, but he would help her because that is what she wanted.

"Well," he began slowly, the drawl slow like molasses on a cold day sending a little shiver up her spine. "Do you want a pretty little trinket, or something practical?"

"Um, I guess practical?"

"Get them a diaper service then." He looked down at his energetically rocking daughter. "When this one was born, there was nothing wrong with her plumbing and we went through so many diapers."

"Dad!" Teeny wrinkled her nose. "You're disgusting."

"It was your diapers," he replied, making a face back at her.

Chloe felt a twinge as she thought about a young Travis and Caroline, excitedly preparing for their new arrival. It was hard not to feel envious of that special time they had shared. "Maybe we could get something a little less practical?"

"Get the baby something that it can use in about three, maybe six, months from now. Everyone always buys lots of tiny stuff, but you only use that for about a month if you're lucky. Then the baby has nothing."

She pondered the wisdom of his words. She'd always known Travis was a practical no-frills man, but she hadn't realized just how far that went till now. She smiled. At least she knew any advice he gave wouldn't be frivolous. "But the newborn stuff is all so tiny and cute."

"And you'll get lots of it when we have our own baby." He cleared his throat, sudden awareness of what he'd said making him red. Chloe's eyes went wide at his words. *Our own baby.* "I meant you have your own baby." His eyes slid away as Chloe continued to stare at him, completely thrown by what he had said.

Oblivious, Teeny continued to rock. "Can we get them one of these chairs?"

Relieved for a change in subject, Chloe laughed, albeit a little breathlessly. "No, I don't have that much to spend on them."

In the end, they decided to buy little outfits starting at newborn and going up several sizes to cover the first year of Edward's life. As she signed the card in the parking lot, Chloe looked down at all their names in a neat little line at the bottom. *Just like a family,* she thought, glancing up to where Travis was making sure Teeny had fastened her seatbelt. *We look just like a family.*

TRAVIS HAD SURPRISED the girls by deciding to have dinner while they were in town. It had been nice, and Chloe continued her fantasy by pretending that this was what it would be like if they really were a family.

The night sky was bright with stars and country music played on the radio as the little group drove back to Affinity Ranch. Teeny's eyes had grown heavy until they finally drooped shut and the youngster fell asleep. At last, the barn with its bunkhouse was illuminated in the truck's headlights. Chloe had to fight against the pang of regret that the evening was over and this was, in fact, not her family. She unfastened her seatbelt and shifted her weight to face Travis better. "Thank you for coming shopping with me. I had a great time." Her voice was soft so as not to disturb the slumbering girl.

"I did, too." His features were a study in contrast, the light from the dashboard setting it to shadowy crevasses and peaks. He peeked at his daughter. "I think Teeny would say she had a good time too, if she was awake."

"She loved those rocking chairs."

"I know. It was kinda concerning by the end." He unclicked his seatbelt. "I'll walk you to the barn."

"Oh, you don't have to." Chloe quietly opened her door, her foot already reaching for the gravel outside.

"I know. And I'm still going to walk you to your door." He looked at her over the hood of the truck as he walked around to her side. "What kind of gentleman doesn't walk a girl to her door at the end of a date?"

Chloe's tummy turned to a quivering mess at his words. "Is that what we just did? Go on a date?"

His mouth quirked as he took her hand and began to escort her to the barn. "Yep. I took my two favorite girls shopping and then to dinner. That qualifies as a date in my book."

"Our first actual date," Chloe marveled. "And I didn't realize until it was all over."

"Maybe I need to try harder for our next one."

"So that means there's going to be a next one?"

Travis's face was serious as he drew to a halt at the first step to the bunkhouse. "I know I've done this all back to front. Usually you go on the dates and then have the quiet evening in, having dinner and talking over dishes."

Chloe reached for his other hand. "I wouldn't change a thing."

"Me neither. I know I'm too old for you, but that doesn't seem to scare you the least bit. Somehow, I got lucky, and I still don't know what you see, but you do see something in me." His voice roughened. In the shadowy light of the barn, Chloe couldn't see his face clearly, only the outline of his features. "I don't want to hide being together anymore from Teeny. I don't want to hide that I'm in love with you."

His words were so deep and intense it left her dazed and trembling. "I love you, too," she said, her voice husky with emotion. "I love Teeny, too."

"And I love you even more for that." As if he couldn't fight the desire anymore, he lowered his head and kissed her. Chloe wholeheartedly gave into the love she felt for this man.

IN THE TRUCK, sleepy grogginess vanished, replaced with a ferocious sense of betrayal. As the couple at the door of the barn luxuriated in their declarations of love, Teeny watched on, jealousy searing her young heart.

CHAPTER 15

The click clacks of her boots sounded extraordinarily loud as she made her way into the ward. Try as she might, even on tiptoes, her steps seemed too noisy for the serene room. Everything about it whispered calm and very sterile. Megan lay peacefully in bed watching the television that hung suspended from the ceiling as beside her, in a clear plastic crib, her baby lay wrapped up into a neat little bundle.

"Good morning," Chloe whispered, scared she would somehow ruin the tranquility.

"Hi." Megan gave her a tired smile. "It's okay, you can talk normally. Are these for me?" She gestured to the arrangement of flowers, a blue balloon bobbing in the air attached, and the large gift bag Chloe held in her hands.

"Yes, they're from Travis, Teeny and me." Chloe found a spot on the nightstand and placed the floral arrangement down before handing the bag to Megan. She peered down at the tiny being, content in his crib, as Megan began to take out each of the little outfits, exclaiming over the cute factor of each one. "He's so cute and tiny. Look at that little squished nose."

"Well, he didn't feel so bloody tiny when I was trying to push him out, I can tell you. This gift is bloody amazing. Thank you so much. Come here and give me a hug."

Megan held her arms out commandingly and Chloe willingly complied, albeit gently.

"So how does it feel to be a mom?"

"It's the scariest and best feeling ever. I know in every fiber of my body that I'd kill for him and, at the same time, he's so fragile and small that I was worried about picking him up to begin with. I just want to do everything right. You know, be the best mom he could want."

Shadows of sadness reflected in the depths of Megan's eyes and Chloe was quick to try and dispel them. "You will be. I mean, look at this little man, all pink and squishy. You made him."

"Well, Carlos likes to think he had something to do with it, too." Megan laughed.

"I guess we can give him some of the credit."

The sadness still lingered around the edges as Megan looked down at her slumbering son, his mouth puckered and making little sucking sounds in his sleep. "I didn't have the best example. I never want to be like that. I never knew moms like Sra Ana actually existed. That's who I want to be like—that's the sort of mom my son deserves."

"I think the fact you worry about not being a good mom means you probably already are. Seriously, look how adorable he is, making that little noise." Chloe gushed over the newborn.

Megan shook her head fondly. "I swear, Chloe, if anyone is meant to be a mom, it's you."

"Yeah, I've always liked babies and kids. Mom used to call me little mother when I was small. I used to always be mothering the other kids." She gave a wry smile at her friend at the amused look she received.

"And now you have Teeny."

"And now I have Teeny," she agreed, still unable to stop her gaze returning to the newborn perfection.

"How is my beautiful wife this morning?"

Chloe turned at Carlos's voice as he swept into the room, his parents only a few steps behind. He gathered Megan in his arms and kissed her gently before settling her against the pillows again. Megan glowed under the pride and love that shone from him and she gratefully accepted the paper cup he handed to her. She took a sip and then looked up at him disappointed.

"This isn't coffee."

"No," Sra Ana agreed, bustling over for a hug. "Caffeine is bad for the baby and we did not think you would appreciate decaf. We got you a nice hot chocolate instead. Is it not delicious? I got one for myself as well."

"Well, I do like chocolate," Megan grudgingly admitted.

"Then we did well." Senhor Edwardo congratulated the others as he took his turn for a hug. "Now, how did my grandson go overnight? Did he give you lots of sleep?"

Chloe felt like an intruder to the intimate family scene that was playing out before her eyes. Happiness for her friend filled her. Megan deserved every molecule of love she was given by the Cabrera's. Maybe one day, under its bright light, some of the pain she carried from her childhood would wash away.

"If you'll excuse me, I need to finish up a few things back at the ranch before I go get Teeny."

"Thank you for visiting and for the gorgeous gifts. Please tell Travis and Teeny I said hi and thank you," Megan said.

"Will do. Bye, Senhor Eduardo and Sra Ana. Congratulations, Carlos, he's gorgeous."

Chloe left the Cabrera's cooing over Edward, feeling a longing to hold a baby of her own in her arms. One day, there might be a little brother or sister for Teeny.

~

CHLOE WATCHED, horrified as the pyramid crumpled, the flyers tumbling to the ground. Beth rushed to the matt when her daughter remained prone on the floor, whimpering in agony. Ms Ruby was asking the girl questions about where it hurt. Teeny stood to one side, her face sullen, fists balled at her hips. After long moments, Beth helped her ashen-faced daughter to her feet and glared at Teeny.

"This is your fault, you stupid little twit." She screamed at her.

"I can't help if it if your daughter can't balance."

Chloe gasped at Teeny's rude reply and leapt to her feet, rushing out to join the fray. "I'm sure she didn't mean that. Say sorry, Teeny."

"I did too mean it." Teeny turned hostile eyes to her. "You're not my mom. You can't tell me what to do."

Hatred snaked across Beth's face. "She's never deserved to be on this squad and today proves it, letting my girl get hurt. I expect you to do something about this, Ms Ruby, or I'll take it further."

Chloe watched Beth lead her hobbling daughter from the room, shocked to see the sullen expression remain on Teeny's face. Ms Ruby sighed beside her. "Teeny, being part of cheer is being a team player. What I saw today, you either made a big miscalculation or you didn't care what happened to your teammate. Don't think it didn't escape my attention that you didn't check to see if she was okay or apologize. I expect more from my girls. If you can't meet those expectations and continue to act this way and be disruptive, I can't have you on my squad. I want you to think about that before you come to the next practice."

Teeny blinked back angry tears. "I don't want to be here, anyway." She stormed from the room.

Devastated at how it was unfolding, Chloe turned apologetically to Ms Ruby. "I'm sure she doesn't mean that, she loves cheer. I just don't know what's gotten into her. This isn't like her."

Ms Ruby's mouth was pressed into a thin line, obviously unimpressed with Teeny's display of petulance. "You better find out what it is. Otherwise, she's off the squad. I like her, and I have fond memories of her mom, but I won't tolerate behavior like that in my team."

Lost at what she could say, Chloe simply nodded before setting off in pursuit of the angry girl.

THE CAR RIDE home would have to go down in history as the most uncomfortable of all time. Nothing but sullen silence. No matter how Chloe tried to get Teeny to talk, the girl simply stared out the window. Finally, Chloe gave up and drove on without speaking. As they turned into the drive, she gave one final attempt. "Teeny, I don't understand what's going on. I'm your friend, please talk to me."

Chloe was taken aback by the look of pure hatred Teeny shot at her. "You're not my friend, you never were. You used me so you could get close to my dad."

Chloe's knuckles turned white on the steering wheel. "Teeny, I don't know what you're talking about. I would never do that." Before the vehicle had stopped moving, Teeny had unbuckled her seatbelt and leapt from the car. Chloe quickly put it into park and followed her. "Teeny," she called.

"I hate you and I wish I'd never met you!" screamed Teeny, rage ripping through her voice.

Alerted of their arrival, Travis came around the corner to greet them and stopped dead in his tracks at the sight and sound of his raging daughter. He looked to Chloe, uncertain what was happening. "Teeny, don't talk to Chloe like that."

Teeny stiffened before turning her furious gaze to her father. "Like what? You're just as bad as her."

Chloe held her hands out trying to calm down the situation. "I think we all need to just take a minute and breathe."

"Stop talking, Chloe. I know what you and Dad have been doing. You're both liars, acting like you're my friend. I hate you!" She ran off into the house crying.

Travis began to follow his upset daughter. "I need to go to her."

"I understand. I never meant for it to turn out like this."

"Neither of us did. She'll come around, you'll see. She'll calm down and I'll talk to her and everything will be okay."

Chloe swallowed down the cold knot of anguish, despair hitting her hard. How had they gotten it so wrong? They'd hurt Teeny not by loving each other, but by hiding it from her. "I hope so." Even to her ears, it didn't sound convincing.

CHAPTER 16

*D*ays that had been filled to the brim now stretched out endlessly for Chloe. Teeny still refused to see her, let alone speak to her, since she had flung her knowledge of their betrayal in their faces. Chloe had only managed to see Travis quickly when Teeny had been at school, but neither had felt right sneaking behind Teeny's back, not when it was the cause for the sad situation they now found themselves in. Except for a handful of phone calls where he had done his best to reassure her that his daughter just needed time to adjust, she had had very little contact with him.

Megan was busy with settling into life with a newborn, and there was no way she was going to bring her current negative energy around that happy little family. Megan deserved to remain wrapped up in her euphoric bubble of new motherhood. Chloe desperately wished Frankie and the twins would return—anything to fill the emptiness.

At the end of each day, Chloe found herself drawn to the youngstock, eagerly testing each other out, bounding and curious. Nova, the eldest of the herd always captured her attention. Now having outgrown the gangly awkward year-ling and two-year-old stage where nothing seemed to grow at the same time, she had now turned into an elegant, leggy filly. A star ready to shine.

"I thought only horses were meant to have long faces?"

Chloe jumped, so caught up in her own maudlin thoughts she hadn't heard Deb's approach. "Yeah, well apparently, they don't have the monopoly on them." She sighed bitterly. "Everything's just turned to complete and utter poo."

"I have a little experience in that. Wanna talk about it?" Deb rested her folded arms on the top rail and squinted against the setting rays of the sun.

"Travis and I were seeing each other, and we hid it from Teeny and now she hates me and never wants to see, hear, or talk to me again. That about covers everything you've missed out on." Chloe could taste the bitterness of each word on her tongue as she spoke.

Deb blew out her cheeks in surprise, caught off guard. "Um, wow. I was not expecting that at all. I thought maybe you missed being on the road or were jealous of the twins. Okay, sorry, I'm still processing."

"Take all the time you need. I've got absolutely zero other places I need to be or people that want to see me."

"Well." Deb blinked rapidly as she gathered her thoughts. "It's no use going over what's happened. It's done, there ain't nothing you can bloody do once the horse has already bolted. What's Travis got to say about it all?"

"Give her space and she will come around. But I don't think she will. You should've seen the look in her eyes, the contempt and hurt at us betraying her like that. I thought we were doing the right thing—we both did. We just wanted to make sure that we knew it was the real deal."

"And is it?" Deb turned keen eyes to her.

"Yeah," Chloe said softly. "At least, it was. Travis even told me he loved me."

"Then why are you bloody here sulking?"

Chloe's spine stiffened. "Excuse me? Did you not just hear me tell you that Teeny wants nothing to do with me?"

"She's a kid. They're dramatic little creatures. Big emotions and little control. What you need to do is figure out a way that if she wanted to change her mind, she could. Right now, even if she wanted to be your friend, she has backed herself into a corner. Like something you both have in common."

"We used to have cheerleading, but she doesn't want me there anymore." It had stung to find out that Beth was now picking Teeny up from school and driving her to squad. Chloe could've understood Sara and she would have been grateful, but Beth? Nothing good was going to come from that set up.

Deb watched Nova frolic, tossing her ebony mane as she ran to the other horses, teasing them, goading them to play. "Sometimes it's all about knowing the right carrot to dangle in front of them."

Chloe followed her gaze to the prancing buckskin. "Teeny loves Nova."

"And Nova is due to be broken in."

"You're a genius, Deb." Chloe's face split into a beaming grin. For the first time in days, she began to think that maybe she would be able to salvage this situation after all. "How can I ever thank you?"

"If you could just repeat that when Megan's around, that's all the compensation I require."

TRAVIS CLEARED AWAY THE DISHES, a twinge of regret that he

had only two places to clear. Most days now, Teeny acted as she had before she'd so brutally rejected the notion of Chloe and him being together. Sometimes she might be a little sulky, but overall, she seemed to have forgiven him. That was till he mentioned Chloe and then she shut down before his very eyes. From the moment the midwife had laid the tiny precious bundle in his arms, he had sworn he would protect her from harm. Guilt rankled his soul to know that it had been him who had caused the biggest wound in her young life since her mother's death.

It was the two of them and, no matter how the pain seared his heart at the thought of losing Chloe, he would always put Teeny's happiness first. He only hoped that she wouldn't ask him to put his own last.

CHAPTER 17

"I'll be back in a few hours to pick you up." Hope and doubt warred on Travis's face. Teeny gave a tight little smile, continuing not to acknowledge Chloe standing there.

Chloe decided not to let herself get drawn in by the girl's attitude. "That will give us plenty of time to work with Nova." She was disappointed when Teeny didn't reply. She reminded herself that she wasn't going to expect anything from Teeny, just hope for the best.

She waved goodbye and then led the way to the round yard. Nova, having realized she was separated from her herd, fretted and paced, her sides already gleaming with sweat. Nova ignored their arrival, continuing her laps.

"She doesn't want to be here." Chloe could almost hear the 'just like me' Teeny probably mentally added.

"Horses aren't like dogs. You can't shower them with love and expect them to come running when you want them to. Most of the time, all a horse wants is to hang out in their paddock with other horses." Chloe opened the gate and gestured for Teeny to enter with her. Nova stood, her pounding heart causing her chest to visibly beat. She snorted as they made their way to the center of the yard. "Easy, pretty girl."

"But she knows us. Why is she acting like this?" Teeny stared back at the filly, mesmerized by her wild beauty. Then, as if remembering she didn't like Chloe, her expression became guarded again.

Disappointed, Chloe tried her best to not let it show as she stood watching Nova. "She does know us, but that doesn't mean this isn't scary for her. It's easy for her to trust us when she has the security of the herd behind her. What we need to do is start talking to each other in the same language, let her know that she can trust us." Chloe gave a flick of the rope she carried, and Nova took off around the perimeter of the pen. "She needs to learn that it is best to work with us, not against us. She's a smart girl, so it won't take her long." The filly continued hell-bent around in circles. "My job is to watch, to look for any signs that she wants to try. That's all we want today." Chloe focused intently, forgetting in the moment that Teeny was hostile to her. Somehow, there was magic between the two of them and the beautiful buckskin filly.

Beside her, she could feel Teeny leaning forward, willing Nova to try. Gradually the horse began to flick an ear, her attention no longer on mad flight, but on the quiet humans in the center of the pen. Chloe dropped her arm, letting her body relax. Beside her, Teeny did the same.

"Good girl," the girl breathed as Nova slowed, finally stopping to face them. Teeny grabbed her arm. "She did it. That's what we wanted her to do, isn't it?" She smiled excitedly up at Chloe. "This is better than Frankie letting me name her."

The pure happiness in the girl gave Chloe hope that maybe they had turned the corner today. Suddenly, like shutters coming down, the girl obviously remembered that she hated Chloe. She glared at her and bolted from the pen, causing Nova to snort in surprise.

Chloe took off after her. "Teeny. Teeny, please talk to me. Your dad and I, we didn't mean to hurt you. We love each other, and we just wanted to take things slow. We didn't hide it from you for any other reason than we wanted to be sure."

Teeny's mad dash abruptly stopped. She stood with her back to Chloe, fists balled at her sides. "I hate you."

Her own pace now slow, Chloe walked softly to stand in front of the troubled youngster. Agony shot through her when she saw the tears streaming down Teeny's face. "When I used to close my eyes, I could see Mom and Dad looking down at me, smiling. Now, when I close my eyes, I can't see her. I see you and Dad instead."

Chloe's heart broke at Teeny's anguish. She reached out to comfort her, to take her in her arms. "I never want to replace your mom."

The girl jerked out of reach. "I hate you. You made me lose Mom!" she screamed, running toward the sound of Travis's truck pulling up.

Travis looked up in surprise as his sobbing, distraught daughter threw herself into his arms. As he gazed over Teeny's head, all Chloe could do was say, "I'm so sorry. So very sorry."

A world of regret flashed between them. There was nothing left to say. Without another word, he bundled Teeny, her anguish now spent, into his truck. With one last glance, a look that encapsulated the impossibility of the situation, he drove off.

TRAVIS GLANCED down at his exhausted daughter, trying to

reassure himself that the worst had passed. "Do you want to tell me about it?"

Teeny sniffled as she gazed out the window. "Why did Chloe have to ruin everything?"

Guilt shot through him at the unfairness that his daughter should pin the blame on Chloe—a good person that's only fault had been to fall in love with him. "She didn't ruin anything. If you want someone to blame, you should blame me."

Silence greeted his pronouncement. Travis resigned himself for a long, uneasy drive home. The sound of his daughter's voice was a quiet whisper as she continued her vigil out the truck window. "I'm scared, Dad."

"Scared of what, honey?"

"I'm scared I'm losing you to Chloe. She's already made me lose Mom." Such a world of hurt in such simple words.

Travis swallowed over the pain her words caused him, his throat thick with emotion. He realized that Teeny had been too young to properly grieve for the loss of her mother when it had happened. Now it was as if she was going through it all over again. "You're never going to lose me. And Chloe doesn't want to take me away from you. She loves you, too. The fact is that she's made me happier than I have been for a long time."

The flash of betrayal in Teeny's eyes burned him to his core. "I thought I made you happy?"

"You do, honey. But Chloe makes me feel a different type of happy. Maybe I've been a little lonely since we lost Mom." He reached across for her hand, holding it tightly. "But you are and always will be my priority. If Chloe and I being together makes you this unhappy, well I guess we just can't be together."

CHAPTER 18

Her heart pounded painfully in her chest, her fingers feeling cold as she gripped them tightly together, watching Travis approach. Chloe could tell from his stooped shoulders and dragging steps that he hadn't come to deliver good news. An ache in the back of her throat made her try to swallow, but even that was difficult. Wetting her dry lips, she smiled sadly at him.

"You don't need to say it. I already know." She pressed her trembling lips tightly together, trying valiantly to hold her tears in.

Looking into his soulful eyes almost destroyed her resolve. Anguished despair swirled in their depths. "I love you. That hasn't changed."

"But sometimes that's not enough," she finished for him, sorrow choking her. "One day, when she's ready to hear it, can you please tell Teeny I love her, too, and I'm sorry?"

"I wish—" His jaw clenched, the muscle in his cheek twitching. "I wish I could make all of us happy."

"I know, but you're doing the right thing. It sucks, but

Teeny needs to know she is the most important thing to both of us."

He closed the last few yards between them and, without a word, gathered her into his strong embrace, holding her as if he never wanted to let her go. A deadweight dropped in her chest, making it impossible to breathe at the realization that he would soon have to let her go and he would never hold her like this again.

"Please," she whispered. "Give me one last kiss and go."

The world blurred as Chloe's heart clenched painfully in her chest, the tears he was unable to shed spilling down her cheeks, his lips softly saying what he could not, and then he was gone.

THE COWGIRL gently lowered the saddle onto the waiting horse, the filly nervously swishing her tail as the unfamiliar weight settled. The woman made a fuss over how clever the horse was before very slowly reaching under for the cinch.

"I always felt a little nervous doing that," admitted Megan, baby Edward in a carrier on her chest as she watched with her friends from the sideline.

"It is a job for the young," Senhor Eduardo agreed.

"It's nice not having to do the breakers anymore," Deb said, Grace beside her trying to see through the rails into the pen.

"Gosh, doesn't she look like Delila, standing there?" Frankie said, shading her eyes. "It seems like a lifetime ago that I came over to ride a champion buckskin mare that some crazy Brazilian chick offered me a ride on."

Gabi smiled at the memory. "So much has changed. There's no way any of us expected the adventures we've had, the men we love. What are we up to now? Four weddings, two babies and men that're still wondering what hit them." She laughed. "Or maybe that's just Joao."

"Did we get old?" Frankie asked. "I don't feel like I am, and then I spend time with the twins. Chloe's not so bad, she has an old head on her shoulders."

"Don't get me started on the twins," groaned Deb. "I can't be the only one that's not exactly upset that they went home to visit their parents."

Sra Ana laughed. "If the twins make you girls feel old, imagine how it is for Senhor Eduardo and me."

"You must feel positively ancient," Gabi agreed. "Oh, Frankie, that reminds me."

"That you're old?" Frankie didn't take her eyes of Chloe, now jumping softly up and down beside Nova, before using her hands to pull down gently on the stirrups. Nova took a few hesitant steps sideways, unsure what to make of her actions. Chloe soothed her and waited for her to stand still again before repeating her actions.

"Very funny. No, you got the part." She quickly ducked behind the safety of her mother.

"Tell me I didn't hear that right." Frankie chased after her nervously giggling friend.

Gabi moved to the other side, holding Sra Ana between the two of them like a shield. "Congratulations! They said the camera loved you."

"What happens if I'm no good?" wailed Frankie.

"All you have to be is you. How hard can it be?" Deb jerked her head toward the pen where Chloe still worked with Nova. "Someone better break the news to her."

"Why?" Megan asked following Deb's gaze.

"She's going to be spending a bloody lot of time holding a bucket."

~

TEENY WATCHED her dad move the peas around his plate with a fork. Somehow, the room didn't seem as brightly lit as it used to. Maybe she needed to ask Dad to fix it or something. Unable to stand the gloom anymore, she plastered a bright smile on her face, determined to make her dad smile.

"Cheer went good today. Ms Ruby wants me to start filling in as top flyer for some of the stunts so I know how to do them. Sue Ellen is going to be allowed to start training soon. You should see her sitting on the sideline all grumpy. I need you to fill in a form, too. There's a competition that we are all busing down for."

She didn't mention that, as soon as the squad had been told about the weekend away, her first thoughts had been how much fun it would be to have a girls' weekend with Chloe and hang out. A feeling that she couldn't describe had left her feeling crummy afterwards. Watching her father now, the same feeling washed over her, chasing her appetite away as well.

"I can do the dishes tonight, Dad," she offered, taking her plate to the sink.

Travis returned from the fog he had been in. "Huh? Oh, it's okay, honey. I don't mind doing them." He joined her at the sink, ruffling her hair. "I'm proud of you, too, doing that flyer stuff. Maybe I'll come to your next practice. I can't promise I'll understand it all, but I'd like to see you in action."

She tried to push down the niggling thought of how Chloe would have high fived her and asked about what the different stunts were and say how much she'd improve. It didn't matter if Chloe wasn't there anymore, she told herself. All her dad and her needed was each other, even if her dad's sadness said otherwise.

CHAPTER 19

It punched her hard in the gut that Teeny wasn't there for this special once-in-a-horse's-lifetime moment as Chloe stood on the mounting block, ready to slide onto Nova's back for the first time.

"Easy girl," she said, but she could have saved her breath. The filly didn't so much as twitch a muscle as she eased herself into the saddle. "Who's my good girl?" Chloe said in a sing song voice, patting Nova on the neck. "That's right, Nova's a good girl."

Giving a cluck of her tongue, Chloe asked the filly to move forward into a walk. She felt her muscles relax as Nova nodded her head gently with each stride she took. Deciding to quit while the going was good, she gave the filly one final pat before dismounting.

"Wow, Nova handled that like an old pro," marveled Savannah. "You've done an awesome job with her."

Chloe beamed at the complement as she walked over, Nova keeping pace with her. "Thanks. I hate to admit it, but I was a bit nervous when Frankie told me I was going to be the one to break her in. She's kinda a big deal around here."

"Well, her parents are big deals, at least," added Ash.

"That too." Chloe laughed. The twins might be quarrelsome, and she knew Deb always sighed in relief when they left to go on the road, but it was hard to feel down when they were around. There was this vibrant energy that crackled through the air whenever they were near. "How was the visit home?"

"The usual. Mom tried to feed us too much and Dad watched football." Savannah's fondly smiling face belied her words.

"At least people smiled at home, not like here," Ash added, scowling at Chloe as if to say it was her fault.

"What do you mean?" Chloe frowned at what she felt was an unfair accusation being leveled at her.

"Only that Travis mopes around the house, all gloom and doom." Ash folded her arms and pretended to be Travis, exaggerating the downturn of her mouth.

"And the sighing," added Savannah. "I swear it's like having an old steam engine in the house."

Chloe felt guilty at how happy the twins' words made her feel. She didn't want Travis to be unhappy—she was living with the same anguish of heartbreak that he was. But now she didn't feel like she was suffering alone. Like, somehow, they were still bonded by their pain.

"How's Teeny?"

"She seems okay. Maybe a little quiet and not eating as much as usual." Ash shrugged her shoulders as if it was nothing to be concerned about.

"Actually, now that I think about it, she seems a little sad," Savannah disagreed, her expression mirroring her concern.

"Well, isn't she the reason for all the sighing and general *woe is me*?" Ash said unkindly.

"That's not fair, Ash," Chloe said sharply. "She's just a kid that's confused and scared that she's losing everyone she loves."

"But she isn't, is she? Her dad still loves her, and you love her, too." Ash refused to back down from her comment.

"Drop it," Chloe growled. Ash fell silent.

Savannah blew out her cheeks as she looked around. "This isn't awkward now or anything. Chloe, Ash didn't mean anything. She's just saying what we're all thinking. Maybe Teeny just needs to get over herself a bit. If she would just think about it a little, about how unhappy she has made you guys, not just herself, then maybe she would change her mind."

Teeny's anguished face tormented Chloe's mind. "It's not that simple."

"Well, I'm sorry for what I said then," Ash grudgingly said, scrunching up her nose like the words left a sour taste in her mouth.

"Me too, Chloe," Savannah quickly added. "I know what we all need."

"I think I can guess, and I like how your mind works." Ash smiled in cahoots with her twin.

"Oh my gosh, did you just give your sister a compliment? This is the longest you two have ever gone without arguing. Well, at least since I've known you. Stop it, it's starting to freak me out." Chloe crossed her arms as she narrowed her eyes, suspicious that the twins were up to something.

"Don't you want to know my idea?" Savannah pouted.

"Yeah, Chloe, it's a bit rude to not even ask," agreed Ash.

Chloe looked into identical green eyes, innocence shining forth from their wide-eyed gazes. "Why do I have the feeling I'm going to regret this? Sure, Savannah, what's this great idea?"

"Girls' Night!" The twins squealed, clapping their hands excitedly.

"Yep, there's the regret hitting me now." Chloe's lips twitched, a smile fighting to break out. "I'm not even going to fight it. It didn't matter what I said last time, I still got talked into going."

"It's really better this way." Savannah held her hands over her heart. "Just give in and go with the flow and I guarantee you will have a great time."

THE TWINS SURPRISED HER WHEN, instead of hitting the clubs, they instead chose to go to a bar. "Some cocktails, a little gossip, and hot guys to look at. That's what we need," Ash simply said when Chloe expressed her surprise. "Sometimes, we can read between the lines, you know. You don't need dancing and dodging hands, you need your girlfriends around you, cocktails and laughter." Chloe was genuinely shocked at the perception she was displaying.

And she was right. The bar was playing honky tonk on the jukebox, the booths had good views of the rest of the bar, and the drinks were delectable creations of yum. Chloe had just reached the right stage of relaxation based on alcohol consumption that made her feel deliciously okay with the world.

"I hate to say this, but you guys were right. This is exactly what I needed."

Ash and Savannah looked smugly at each other. "Did you hear that?" Ash asked with a raised eyebrow.

"I wish I'd recorded it."

"It gets you right in the feels," agreed Ash. They turned to Chloe. "Do you think you can say it again?"

"Very funny." Chloe scanned the crowd. "I can wait if you aren't finished." Her sweeping gaze froze. Shock mixed with dread spiked through her, causing her palms to begin sweating. "You have got to be kidding me! Not again." Sitting at the bar, with the same tattooed, buffed guy from last time, was Beth.

"What's going on?" Both twins craned their necks, trying to spot what was the cause of Chloe's alarm. She quickly filled them in on her troubles with Beth.

Ash frowned once she finally zeroed in on the couple in question. "Hey, Savannah, isn't that?"

"That's what I was thinking, too," agreed Savannah. "Small world—or should I say, small towns."

"What are you guys going on about?" Chloe looked at her friends in exasperation.

"That guy who's with her, he's not from here," Savannah began.

"Well, his cousins are from here, but him and his mom used to live in the same town as us," added Ash.

"Anyway," Savannah picked up the conversation again. "He used to go to school with us. He spent a bit of time in Juvie."

"Last I heard, he was in jail for a DUI and drug possession," Ash said. Chloe's eyes narrowed as she peered at the couple. It didn't make sense. From what Sara had told her, Beth's husband was a successful dentist and she had a huge house in a nice neighborhood. Why would she parade a guy like that around town? Her bladder decided to pick this moment to suggest that she might want to go and find a bathroom fairly soon. Looking around, she was dismayed to discover that it was located directly behind Beth. In fact, she would have to pass her to get to them.

Weighing up how great her need was, she sighed, knowing that she was going to need to go sooner rather than later. "I need to go to the bathroom."

"Wow, that's poor timing. I guess you can always say hi to

her on the way through," Ash cheekily suggested, smiling at the thought.

"That's a good one," Savannah congratulated her sister.

"Thank you. I thought it was good too."

"I liked you both better when you argued all the time. You need to tell me sometime what happened to make you guys stop." Chloe stood and began to shuffle to the edge of the booth.

"It might have been drawn to our attention that all things need to be done in moderation. Just because we enjoy it doesn't mean that everyone around us enjoys listening to it all the time," explained Savannah.

"Who said that?" Chloe asked, straightening her top.

"Deb," Ash said, looking sheepishly away.

Chloe burst out laughing. "I can bet she said something. I'm kinda surprised she took this long. Now, wish me luck." She did her best to keep her gaze straight ahead. *Almost there...* Suddenly, she was launching through the air, only just managing to keep her feet. She glared behind her to find Beth, the picture of innocence.

"Oh dear, you really are a bit clumsy. It's a good thing Teeny isn't related to you, there'd be no chance of her being a cheerleader if she was." Beth smirked. "It's really no wonder that child wants nothing to do with you. You're just like that trash, Sara—worthless."

A haze of red washed over Chloe, blinding her with rage. *How dare this woman say anything about Teeny.* Her fists balled at her side so tightly she could feel her nails digging into the palms of her hands. "I guess you'd know about worthless. Is that why you're here and not at home? Because your husband wants nothing to do with you?"

Beth's look could cut glass. "Oh, he still wants it, but I want my fun to be a little younger." She ran her fingers lightly up her dates arm. "Isn't that right, darlin'?" She turned her icy gaze back to Chloe. "In fact, he's probably in bed right now, dreaming of ways to keep me happy, the poor fool."

Chloe's already low opinion of Beth plummeted to depths she didn't even know were possible. "I feel sorry for him being married to a woman like you."

"I think you'll find that he knows I'm out of his league. He was lucky I even gave him the time of day when we first met, let alone married him."

The sour bile of disgust filled Chloe's mouth. Unable to stomach the conversation any longer, she turned on her heel, heading toward the bathroom. Behind her, Beth laughed. "Say hi to Teeny for me." She slapped her forehead, appearing to suddenly remember something. "Oh, that's right, she doesn't want anything to do with you. I guess I'll say it to her myself when I pick her up for cheer."

Chloe drew in deep breaths, fighting with every fiber of her being not to fly across the distance that separated them and slap the horrible woman silly. Gritting her teeth, she swung open the door into the sanctuary that was the bar's bathroom.

THE CERAMIC OF the bowl was cold against her forehead, providing relief until her stomach clenched again. The acid of her vomit burned the back of her throat and left a horrific taste in her mouth.

A knock on the door interrupted her misery. "Are you okay in there?" asked Mitch through the door.

"I think I'm dying," she groaned, hugging the bowl again.

She grimaced at Mitch's laughter that seemed just a little too loud to her as it pierced her brain like shards of glass. "Mate, I've had a few nights end up like that when I was young. I'll go get Deb."

"Only if she can put me out of my misery."

More laughter caused her to wince under its onslaught. "The only person I know that's bloody qualified to do that is Carlos." Chloe could still hear him chuckling as his footsteps retreated, leaving her in blessed peace.

CHAPTER 20

The wood of the pew in front her was warmly smooth to the touch. The leadlight saints, the jewel bright eyes gazing down, sent dancing rainbows across her hand. Chloe looked around, curiously taking in the holiness of the church. Everywhere were little touches that caused her to marvel. Elegantly carved work on the statuary niches, tall candles, gold crucifixes. The upward thrust of the baldachin over the high altar sent Chloe's eyes heavenward. As her gaze drifted down, she saw the priest smiling at her.

"It's beautiful," she breathed in awe.

"Is this your first time in a catholic church?" he asked without judgement.

Chloe took in his glowing white robes, briefly wondering if it would be rude to ask how he kept them so white. "Yes."

"When I was a novice, I served at the Sao Francisco Church. When the sun shone in on clear days, the gold shone so brightly it blinded you." He smiled fondly at the memory from his youth. "If you like Baroque architecture, I would highly recommend a visit to see it."

"I'll have to google it," promised Chloe.

Megan and Carlos walked into the church, baby Edward in a snowy white baptismal gown. Chloe didn't think she had ever seen Megan look so completely happy before. Carlos looked fit to burst with pride.

"You'll have to excuse me. I need to speak to the parents." The priest apologized as he left.

Entering behind the proud parents came Sra Ana and Senhor Eduardo and the rest of the extended family, both adoptive and real. Chloe settled back in her seat and breathed in the particular brand of serenity the church filled her with.

"Wow, this is one heck of a church." Ash seated herself beside her, Savannah close on her heels.

"We thought you might want some support, you know, since this is the first time you've seen Teeny and Travis since..." Savannah left it hanging.

"You know, since you guys broke up," Ash helpfully added.

"Yes, thank you, Ash. Like Chloe needs you to smack her over the head with it. I'm pretty sure she knew what I meant."

"Well, maybe she didn't. Did you think about that? Maybe Chloe was sitting there wondering what on earth you were talking about."

"She's not dumb."

"I think you're dumb."

"Real mature, Ash."

"That didn't take long, did it?" Chloe rolled her eyes heavenward.

"What do you mean?" chorused back at her.

"The not fighting thing. And yes, I knew what Savannah meant. Simple Simon knew what she meant."

Both twins' mouths formed perfect o's, but before she could say more, Travis and Teeny made their way down the aisle, his gaze steadfastly fixed ahead of him. Her eyes hungrily drunk in the sight of him, his neatly combed hair and freshly pressed clothes. She was near enough that she could smell wafts of his aftershave. She took deep breaths, breathing it in. Anguish hammered through her when, for the briefest of moments, his gaze flickered to hers, the bond they had shared flaring to life, the naked longing painful in its intensity before he quickly extinguished it by looking away. Teeny followed the direction of her father's look and Chloe found herself on the receiving end of a stare that she couldn't quite decipher.

"Are you okay?" asked Savannah, peering around Ash and blocking Teeny from view.

"It doesn't really matter how I feel. Today is about baby Edward and Megan and Carlos and, well, the whole family. I'll worry about how I feel tomorrow."

To validate her words, she attempted to tamper down any thoughts or feelings that didn't directly relate to the baptism. No matter how far she pushed them down, her broken heart refused to be quietened. Sighing, she looked straight ahead as the kindly priest called the parents and godparents forward.

A hush fell over the expectant crowd as the baptism looked set to begin. From her side, she heard a gentleman's voice. "Excuse me, miss, is this spot taken?"

She heard Savannah give a quick, "No."

"Squish up a bit, we need to make more space," Ash whispered beside her, Chloe shuffling over a few inches as she complied.

At the front, near the baptismal font, Megan and Carlos smiled at something the priest said and Megan gestured for someone to join them. Frankie, Luciano, Mitch and Deb joined them at the front. Megan had been very clear in the weeks leading up to the baptism that the four of them were as much family to Edward as Gabi and Joao in their official titles as Aunt and Uncle. To consolidate her feelings, she had asked them to be their baby's godparents.

"What name do you give this child?" asked the priest.

"Edward." Carlos and Megan solemnly intoned.

"Are the parents and godparents willing and able to fulfill their duties to bring this child up in the Christian faith?"

The assembled loved ones all answered affirmatively, smiling down at baby Edward. The priest gently made the sign of the cross on the baby's forehead and began to read a passage from the ornate Bible he held. In the front row, Chloe could see Sra Ana dab at her eyes with a lacy white handkerchief, Senhor Eduardo looking suspiciously close to tears. The love in the room was so tangible it was like a living, breathing being in the church. Chloe felt like, if she reached out, she might somehow be able to touch it. The thought of love sent her mind careering toward thoughts of Travis. Determinedly, she brought her attention back to the present.

The priest gently pulled down the neckline of Edward's white robe before smearing some oil on the infant's neck. When Megan had shown them the exquisite gown earlier, she had proudly told them it was the same one that both Gabi and Carlos had worn. The priest, smiling gently at the squirming baby, moved closer to the font and began blessing the water. He gestured for Megan and Carlos to bring Edward and hold him over the basin. Twice, he poured the water over the baby's head and said his name. Judging from Edward's reaction, he either wasn't a fan or the water was chilly. A third time, the water was poured, this time the priest intoning, "I baptize you in the name of the Father and of the Son and of the Holy Spirit. Amen."

From Chloe's engrossed point of view, after that, it all moved along quite quickly. He rubbed some more oil on the top of Edward's head and then lit a candle from one of the biggest candles she had ever seen. And just like that, the world welcomed another Christian to the fold.

TEENY HAD BEEN agog at the pageantry of Edward's baptism and, as her father slowly moved through the crowd, she was still filled with a tingling energy that she hadn't felt before. She waved at Gracie through the throng of people, excited that she would be able to catch up with her at the reception. Although younger at four to her more mature seven, Teeny had missed hanging out with her. Beside her, she felt her dad stiffen and saw Chloe brush past in the crowded aisle.

Chloe had always seemed to glow with this sort of inner light, this thing that made you feel good from just being around her. Now, she seemed dull and washed out, her eyes sad and … something else. Teeny thought hard about it. She looked like that time Sue Ellen from cheer had fallen over and broken her arm, like something was really hurting her. Chloe glanced at Travis. Teeny thought she looked like she was going to cry before pushing past the people in front of her and disappearing from the building.

Her cousins shook their heads sadly at her dad and quickly followed Chloe. She looked up at her father. His eyes looked exactly like Chloe's had, his mouth downturned as he blinked rapidly. She hated seeing him like this and, if she was a teeny tiny bit honest with herself, she didn't like seeing Chloe like that either. She had, after all, once been her favorite person in the whole world after Dad.

Thoughtfully, she sucked on her cheek as she reached out to hold her father's hand, reassured when he squeezed it back. Maybe she didn't hate Chloe after all.

CHAPTER 21

The tree stood sentry over the party, its gnarled limbs reaching out as it held its massive canopy up. Chloe marvelled at is age, its trunk so stupendous several of them could link arms and only just embrace its girth. Somehow, she felt in her bones that this tree had seen its fair share of tragedy and happiness. Mainly happiness since the Cabreras had been custodian of it, she decided. Today was certainly a case in point, the celebration of the newest Cabrera's baptism. If she thought Sra Ana and Frankie had thrown a lavish party before, nothing compared to the outright decadence of the spread today.

She stood in the shade of the behemoth with the twins, sipping on a glass of cold lemonade. Both the girls had laughed when she had shuddered at the thought of the mimosas they drank. After her last disastrous date with alcohol, she had declared she was never going to drink anything stronger than soda ever again.

"Hello, Chloe." Bryce ambled over. "I believe I need to thank your friend for her kindness in allowing me to sit beside her back at the church." He picked up Savannah's hand and kissed it. Savannah blushed under the gentlemanly attentions of the cowboy businessman. Ash stood wide-eyed, unsure what exactly was going on, but not liking it either way.

Chloe's brows shot skyward at his actions. "I guess since you've already started kissing her, I should introduce you. Bryce, the young lady's hand you have a hold of is Savannah, and the one that looks exactly the same is Ash." She gave him a little smirk. "All I want to say is good luck with that."

Bryce smiled good naturedly. "I do enjoy a challenge, especially one as sweet as this." Savannah giggled girlishly, surprising Chloe. Ash snorted in disgust. "Can I get ya'll ladies a drink?"

"We'll both have mimosas." Ash thrust her empty glass into his hand. Bryce was nothing but unflappable at her action. "Three mimosas it is."

"Two." Chloe quickly corrected, holding out her two fingers for emphasis.

"Nothing for you, then? Water, lemonade?"

"Our Chloe has turned her back on liquor. The girl has one bad night out and that's it, she kicks it out of her life forever. Savannah and I aren't quitters." Ash winked at her sister.

"I've found alcohol to be a fickle mistress, but like any great lady, it's best to treat her with respect." He touched the brim of his hat. "I'll be right back."

"Good Lord, who is that adorable hunk of cowboy?" asked Savannah the minute Bryce was out of earshot.

"That's Bryce Dougson, one of Frankie's and Luciano's major sponsors. He also used to sponsor Joao as well. Now, Joao just works for him."

"Hang on a minute," Ash said, looking after the departing Bryce. "The man I just demanded get me a drink like some sort of servant, is the Bryce Dougson? CEO of Black Angus

Western Wear and, like, a million other companies, consistently in the top ten most eligible bachelors in the country? That Bryce Dougson?"

Chloe shrugged her shoulders uncommittedly. "If you say so? I only know him as a sponsor. The others are pretty friendly with him, so they might know more." Her eyes drifted across the crowd, unerringly drawn to Travis. His eyes met hers, triggering a bittersweet knot of pain inside her. She wondered if she would ever feel whole again.

"Two mimosas for the ladies." Bryce gallantly offered the drinks and pulled a flask from his jacket pocket. "And for the gentleman." He unscrewed the lid and brought it to his lips. Chloe's hand snaked out, intercepting its path. The little group watched in surprise as she gulped down a swig, the fiery liquid causing her to cough and splutter. Bryce pounded her on the back. "Easy there, tiger. This brew ain't for beginners."

"What has gotten into you?" Ash looked at her like she had suddenly grown two heads.

Savannah looked over her shoulder in the direction Chloe had been staring before her sudden leap into alcoholism. Enlightenment dawned on her face. "Ah."

Before she could say more, Senhor Eduardo called for everyone to come to the table for lunch. And what a table it was. Several long rectangular tables had been joined together and covered in white tablecloths, burlap running down the spine. Little blue stuffed bunny rabbits dotted the table. Bryce, ever the Texas gentleman, held Savannah's chair for her before taking the seat beside her, leaving Ash to sit several seats away.

"Unbelievable. Why is she getting all the attention and I'm not?" Ash muttered angrily to Deb.

"Maybe it's because she's better looking than you," suggested Deb innocently.

"We're identical twins."

"Are you sure? Cause Bryce doesn't seem to think so." Deb smirked into her drink at the outraged look Ash directed at her. Chloe would have laughed at their exchange if she hadn't found herself seated directly opposite Travis and Teeny. Her heart froze in her chest and her appetite, already miniscule, disappeared completely.

"I don't—" She tried to find more words, but no sound, save the ragged drawing of breath, emerged. "I need to go." Tears blurring her vision, she ran, her pain making her feel like a wounded animal desperately seeking refuge to lick its wounds.

TEENY WATCHED the distraught Chloe flee the table. Seconds later, Deb followed her. Confused at what was happening, she looked up at her father. "Dad, is Chloe okay?" Dad's face was pale under his hat, his eyes strained toward where Chloe had disappeared. She couldn't be sure, but it seemed like her dad wanted to go after her. When he still didn't answer, she tugged on his sleeve. "Dad?"

"Yes, honey?" his voice sounded distant.

"I don't want you to be sad anymore and I think the only way you won't be is if you can hug Chloe." She scrunched up her face in thought. "If I think really hard about it, I think Mommy would want you to be happy and she isn't here anymore to do that and I can only make you kid happy, not grown up happy. I'm not scared or mad anymore, and I can't think of anyone that I would want to be my stepmom more than Chloe, so maybe you should go and give her a hug. She seems so sad, too."

Her dad looked at her. She was pretty sure that he was

proud of her, even if he looked like he was about to cry. "Are you sure?"

Teeny nodded. "Yep."

He wrapped his arms around her, and she knew that he would always love her no matter who else became part of their family. "I love you so much. You know that, right?" His voice sounded strange, like he had something stuck in his throat.

"I know. You need to hug Chloe, just like you hugged me. I'm sure she'll feel a lot better if you do. Are you scared, Dad? I can come with you if you like?"

"I think I'd like that very much." Teeny slipped her hand into her father's. "Let's go give Chloe a hug."

THE DESPAIR BURST from her in great waves of agony. Chloe's knees were pulled into her chest and her arms tightly wrapped around them as if to stop herself from being pulled apart by the raw emotion.

"Let it all out." Deb rubbed her back, giving what comfort she could. "Soon, your heartbreak will start to fade until it's nothing but a silvery old scar."

"You don't understand. How I feel about Travis, I'll never feel like that about someone again. He was my soulmate."

"Never is a long time, and you're young. It doesn't feel like it now, but you will get through this."

"I'd prefer she doesn't replace me," Travis said from where he stood awkwardly at the doorway, twisting his hat about in his hands. At his side, Teeny became distressed at the sight of Chloe's anguish and began to cry. He wrapped his arm around his sobbing daughter. "Can we come in? There are some things we need to talk about."

Deb looked between the somber cowboy, the sobbing

woman, and the crying youngster and knew when a situation was beyond her ability to handle. "I guess nothing you say is going to make this worse." She gave Chloe a hug. "I'm going to make myself a coffee. If you need me, I'll just be outside."

Deb had barely made it out of the door before Teeny threw herself on the bed and wrapped her arms around Chloe. "I'm sorry, Chloe. Please don't cry anymore."

Chloe managed to pull her arms free to bring them around Teeny. Her little body quivering, Teeny let out her pain and guilt over the hurt she had caused. The bed springs squeaked as Travis joined them on the bed. Chloe raised puffy bloodshot eyes to his, her grief still visible in the tears that ran down her face. Between them, his daughter quietened to sad hiccups.

"I'm tired, Travis, of feeling this way. Like my heart is dead inside of me. It hurts, and I just want it to stop. How do I figure out how to stop loving you when all I wanted to do was love you both?"

"I hope you never do." He wrapped his strong arms around them both. It felt to Chloe like they were the two people he loved most in the world. "I love you. I might have been a stubborn fool to spend so long fighting it, but I knew you were special the moment I met you."

"I don't want to come between you guys, I never did."

"I know that, and Teeny knows that. She loves you just as much as I do. I want to be a family with you. Teeny and I want to be a family with you," he corrected himself, hope quietly replacing the anguish of before.

Chloe pulled back to look down at the now quiet girl in her arms, the youngster's tears having left her exhausted. "Is that true?"

"I'm sorry for everything." Teeny's bottom lip quivered and Chloe feared she might start crying again. She gave her a tight squeeze.

"I never want you to feel bad for feeling how you feel. You were grieving your mom. I would never try to replace her, but maybe you could let me be here for you, too?"

Teeny hugged her back. "Now, when I close my eyes, I see Dad dancing with you and me, but I also know Mom is smiling down at us. She's happy."

"Oh, Teeny." Chloe's throat thickened with emotion. "That's a beautiful picture to carry around inside you."

Teeny looked up at her father. "Do you think our hugs worked?"

Travis smiled, the crinkles around his eyes that had been gone for so long now back. "I think our hugs worked just fine."

"I think maybe you and Chloe want to do some of that kissy stuff, too. Do you think Deb would make me a hot chocolate if I asked?"

"I'm sure she will," Chloe said, her heart beginning to flutter in her chest.

"Oh, and Dad?"

"Yeah, honey?"

"Don't make Chloe cry again, okay?"

Travis's eyes glowed, never taking them off Chloe's face as he smiled. "I promise to try to never make her cry again." Apparently pleased with his response, she left the two of them alone.

Chloe suddenly felt shy around him, like they were about to kiss for the first time. Travis didn't seem to suffer from the same emotions as he took her in his strong arms. "I am never going to let anyone, or anything, get between us again," he vowed. "I love you."

"I love you, too." As his lips caressed her, she let all her feelings flow through them. She gave him all of her cowgirl love.

"You'd have been proud of how beautiful Teeny looked standing beside her father, just like a fairy princess with the flowers in her hair. She was so excited, too. She just about exploded with pride that she was asked to get ready with us girls and then dashed off to help Travis get ready. Your daughter is an amazing human being, she has so much love in her heart now that she can hear it speak to her again." Chloe smiled at the thought of her daughter—it had been agreed between the three of them that there would be no step about it. "My mom didn't even get halfway down the aisle before she started crying and that set off all the girls. I think Frankie was the worst, but she cries at the drop of a hat. I'm so glad I asked the makeup artist to put waterproof mascara on everyone." She giggled, suddenly remembering. "I haven't even told you the best bit. The makeup artist knows that cow, Beth—I told you about her— anyway, she had some juicy gossip. Turns out her husband kicked her out of that flash house she lived in when he found out about her and her toy boy. The best bit? He's now dating

Sara. Apparently they've known each other since high school but just kinda lost touch."

"Chloe!" Teeny came careening around the corner, the ribbons in her floral wreath flying out behind her as she bunched up the skirt of her dress to go faster. Chloe smiled at the sight of the pink cowboy boots, love for this complicated child flowing from her already full heart. "Dad says it's time to cut the cake."

"Tell him I'll be right there," she promised.

"Well, don't take too long. Frankie told me it has three different types of chocolate in it."

"I won't." She smiled as Teeny scampered away. She raised her glass of lemonade in salute to the picture of Caroline. "I promise you will never be forgotten. Thank you for letting me share your family." As she walked away, she could feel Caroline smiling down at her, sharing her cowgirl love.

THE END

IF YOU LOVED, *A Cowgirl's Love* sign up for my newsletter to get exclusive chapters and bonus prequel. Not to mention all the news and releases first.

Now, turn the page as the Affinity Stud Ranch story continues with Ash….

A COWGIRL'S movie star

A COWGIRL'S MOVIE STAR - SNEAK PEEK

"*I* don't think we can wait any longer for Frankie, so let's get this meeting started. The twins are running a bit late, too. It took them longer than they anticipated getting home from the rodeo last night. Firstly, Kirk will be arriving in"—Gabi made a show of checking her watch—"exactly three days' time." Excited chatter erupted around the table. Gabi smiled smugly, enjoying the reaction.

A sudden crash of phone and car keys hitting the floorboards silenced the room. "I'm sorry I'm late," Frankie babbled, scooping to collect her things. "Um, Gabi, I need to talk to you."

"Sure thing, let's finish this meeting first and then I'm all yours," Gabi promised, returning to her captive audience. "As I was saying, Kirk will be arriving in three days to begin shadowing Luciano, learning his mannerism and the boys are also going to show him how to be a convincing bull rider. It will also give Frankie a chance to start learning lines and scenes with him." Gabi looked at Frankie in disbelief. "Do you actually have your hand up to ask me a question?"

Frankie nodded, letting her hand drop. "Um, there might be a slight hitch to your plan?" She scrunched her face up anxiously.

"If the boys are being difficult, I'll talk to them. Luciano promised, and Joao will do what I tell him. Kirk has spent the last three months working with a dialect coach to get Luciano's speech patterns right." She turned to Chloe. "Travis is still on board to give him time on the bulls?"

"Sure is."

"Um, Gabi," Frankie said hesitantly shuffling her feet. Gabi noted she still hadn't taken a seat.

"Frankie, are you going to sit down? I'm getting a sore neck looking up at you," Gabi said. Frankie swallowed, finally seating herself and mumbled something incoherently. "I didn't quite catch that?"

"I'm sitting right next to her and I've no bloody idea what she said either," agreed Deb. "What is wrong with you today? You're acting weirder than usual."

Frankie cleared her throat. "I said they're going to have to cast another Frankie."

"What?" exploded Gabi in confusion. "It's a bit late to be backing out now."

"But you're perfect as Frankie," said Chloe.

"It's like she was born to play it, really," agreed Deb. "Anyway, we've already organized Chloe to have time off from the ranch and we've even gotten her a nice new bucket to hold."

Chloe gave Deb a dirty look. "Thanks."

"Don't mention it."

"I'm pregnant." The sound of a pin dropping would have been deafening in the silence that followed Frankie's quiet statement.

"Are you sure?" Gabi leaned forward, peering at her friend's stomach as if she had x-ray vision.

"Got it confirmed this morning. It's why I was late."

Deb finally gathered her wits. "Oh my gosh. I'm so bloody happy for you!" She gathered her friend in a bear hug, thumping her on the back before remembering her delicate condition and letting her go.

"Edward won't be the baby of the family anymore." Megan rocked on her chair slightly as her son slept soundly in her arms.

"Wait until Sra Ana finds out," Chloe said, her eyes wide at the thought.

"She's going to be eyeball-deep in babies and kids soon and loving it," agreed Deb. "Have you told Luciano yet? What did he say?"

Frankie's smile was tender. "He told me that he didn't think he could love me more, but that I had proven him wrong. He is very excited to be a papai." She glanced hesitantly up at Gabi. "It's okay, isn't it? I mean, it wasn't planned, but…" She left the words hanging.

Gabi smiled joyously at her friend. "Another baby. This movie is nothing compared to that. The producers will just have to find someone else. I wonder who."

"If you'd just listened to me, we would've been here hours ago." Savannah's voice floated angrily through the door. The twins were obviously back home.

"Excuse me for needing to stop. I thought I was going to die."

"You ate too much fried food and you had gas." Savannah curled up her lip in derision as the twins entered the room.

Ash pressed her hand into her side. "It could've been my appendix. I could've ended up in hospital, no thanks to you."

"Oh my gosh, you're such a darn drama queen. It's like you're always in the darn movies."

Gabi looked across to Frankie, a smug smile on her face. "Perfect."

. . .

Ash's story, A *Cowgirl's Movie Star,* available on Amazon and Kindle Unlimited

ACKNOWLEDGMENTS

A debt of gratitude to my editor Rebekah Groves for her patience with me.

Another big thanks to Megan from Designed with Grace for her cover design. Who knew it was so hard to get pictures of hot cowboys that were wearing shirts.

To my amazing beta readers and street team, you guys rock and I couldn't do it without you

A cowgirl's billionaire

Release Dec 2020

Christmas Standalone Books

Boots and Mistletoe

ABOUT THE AUTHOR

Edith MacKenzie or Eddie Mac to her friends is an author of sweet and wholesome contemporary cowboy romance. They say in literary circles to write what you know, and Eddie has certainly taken that to heart. Before embarking on a writing career, she trained horses professionally and brings that wealth of knowledge to her writing.

Now a mum to a boy and girl, as well as wife, she delights with her tales of strong cowgirls and their adventures in finding love. When not weaving the love stories of her characters, she enjoys hanging out with her family and animals, as well as reading, fishing and camping.

Just remember—once a cowgirl, always a cowgirl.

facebook.com/EddieMacAuthor
instagram.com/edith_mackenzie_author
amazon.com/Edith-MacKenzie
bookbub.com/profile/edith-mackenzie

GLOSSARY OF AUSSIE SLANG

Now everyone knows that cobbers from the Land Down Under speak the Queen's English, but if you don't know to Tracky Daks from your Servo, I've put together a quick little cheat sheet.

A few stubbies short of a six pack - Crazy

Ankle Bitter - Small child

Arvo - Afternoon

Blind - Intoxicated

Bloody - Very. Used to extenuate a point

Bloody oath - Yes or its true

Bludger - Someone who is lazy

Buggered - Exhausted

Cark it - Die

Choccy Bikkie - Chocolate cookie

Clucky - Feeling maternal

Crook - Feeling sick

Daks - Trousers e.g. Tracky Daks are tracksuit pants

Dog's breakfast - Messy (does not relate to food), a bit of a shambles

Dry as a dead dingo's doing - Exceptionally dry

Flat out like a lizard drinking' - Not doing very much at all

Grog - Alcohol

Hit the frog and toad - Hit the road, get going

Man's not a camel - A man gets thirsty and would indeed like the beverage you are offering him

Mate - Friend or conversely could be someone you barely know

Nay, Yeah - Yes

Pull the wool over someone's eyes - To trick or mislead someone

Reckon - For sure

Ripsnorter - Can also be interchanged with beaut, bonza. Someone doing something exceptionally good

Servo - Petrol Station

Six one way, half a dozen the other - Undecided

Sparrow Fart - Before the crack of dawn. Very, very early in the morning

Stone the flamin' crow - An utterance of surprise of annoyance

Struth - God's truth. Used to express surprise or dismay

She'll be right - Everything is going to okay

Tell 'em they're dreaming - Is never in a million years going to happen

Tighter than a fish's bum - Said person is very frugal with their money

To blow smoke up someone's bum - To give praise that might make the other person cocky or overly confident

Up yourself - Stuck up

Ute - Pickup Truck

Whoop whoop - Middle of nowhere

Wrap ya laughing gear 'round that - Eat this

Yarn - To talk or tell tall tales

Yeah, nay - No

You bloody ripper - Very good, a job well done

www.ingramcontent.com/pod-product-compliance
Lightning Source LLC
Chambersburg PA
CBHW021202110726
47900CB00002B/695